All rights reserved.
©Fallen Angel Am I ©Martin Sigournay
©Fallen Angel Am I is part the series of ©The Order Of Ezekial.

First Edition October 2016

α

The Beginning

I was always told to live my life like it's the last day on this planet. I wish it was... The hunger grows and no matter how I try to satiate. It just keeps coming back.
I've tried everything vegetables, animals, insect but my mouth craves otherwise.
I keep thinking; what would my kids say if I gave up? Perhaps I can find a cure and go back... The question is, would they take me back? How long, have I been away?
I spend my nights searching for the one in that church. I see her in my mind; as though pulling me to take a life to simply relieve this pain. I feel drawn and lean. At least when I go looking for my own kind, I find a few have not given in. They've tried everything to take the pain away by finding a purpose, but I can see in their eyes that they are losing the battle, as I most certainly am.

Where are my manners? I'm John; well, it is now! I should at least tell you what has happened so far and for that I should start at the beginning...

It was always my greatest fear; to lose my family and friends, come to think about it my second worst fear, was losing my sight but I have to admit, it would be a blessing now.
This is how much I remember of how it all started.

I remember, I am running, being chased by something. My heart pounding, my throat; filling with bile.
I try to go faster than I can because behind me, I can hear it panting, its breathing rhythmical; as though it is just a morning jog, it does on the off chance.
I don't know how but I knew exactly what it was. I'd seen something similar in my dreams. It was a Werewolf.

In the back of mind I knew I couldn't keep up the pace, I wasn't going to outrun the beast but still I tried. Under bridges and over the plains I ran. I was being spurred on by my fear.

Eventually I came to a wide river and there was my option.
Find out if it wanted polite conversation or get wet. There wasn't a choice. With both feet; I jumped and began to swim like I had never done before. The cold engulfed my body; my lungs cramping up as I kept pushing and pushing. Telling my body not to give up!
I had been in the water a long time; my body was ready to fail.
The water started getting shallower; until I could touch the bottom with my water soaked shoes. I raised my body out of the freezing water.

I was in town; the lights of the midnight gloom were arrayed from the streetlamps. As I got out I began to walk as though I were constipated with the countless amount of water, which was still in my clothes. Nothing could have followed me this far...

Yet as I turned to check; it was there just over the water from where I was and I could see that it was already trying to work out how to get over to me.

There was a church nearby; I knew the padre and I was sure of sanctuary. My legs didn't want to move but I made them. I stumbled over the stairs, careered through the door to find what I thought was a sermon being taken.

I found myself a seat and put my head between my hands to free the feeling of the blood rushing through my body. Next to me sat a beautiful young lady, her eyes covered by tinted glasses, her long brunette hair hung perfectly; her teeth... now that was the odd bit, they were pointed. I went to get up but all of a sudden the padre was in front of me. I could see his face but it was not the padre I knew; his eyes bear down upon me like the dark of the night, his robes dark red...

Oh my god, what was he? My heart sank. I sat back. I knew that I wasn't

going to get away. The woman beside me turned to the padre and smiled.
"I'll take this one!"

Then without notice she grabbed my chin and turned it ever so carefully as though not to break me, or should I say as though she cared about me. Her breath was cool yet soothing against my burning skin, it was almost erotic.

Then the dull feeling as the teeth punctured my skin. Strange at first, it felt like an injection, then a dull pain; that kind you feel when a large object penetrates into your skin like a knife. You know... That first initial pain, then anything after that doesn't seem real because your body refuses to accept it's there.
There was also that feeling of the drawing of the coursing hot warm blood; the same one you get when you try and give blood to fast... Everything went dark!

The next thing I knew, I was still sat in the pews of the church; but no one was with me. The sun was close to rising, I knew only one thing. I had to be out of the sun.

I headed out of the church towards my uncle's air raid bunker.
I knew he still used it; now and then too hide and smuggle things, it was always dark. The security monitors would allow me to check when the sun goes down.

He found me there, sat in front of his monitor. At first; his eyes fell on my puncture wounds, then to my face. His face filled with pity rather than disgust. It was not what I was expected. He held his arms out for me and I fell into them; tears flowed from my eyes. I had no strength. All I could do was weep.

Finally he sat me down and looked me square in the eyes and explained that I could no longer stay in his shelter. I would get the craving and that I would become a danger to the family. I knew somehow he was right. He fed me that evening on raw steak, which in some way made me feel a bit more whole and yet, not.

As I went that evening I asked him to tell the rest of the family that I had died and to make up a way to bury me. I did not want any of them, to come looking for me, I didn't want them to see what I had become.
As I began to flee that night I could not help but pass by my old house, I had moved into it two years ago with my wife and child. There in front was everything that I had earned, everything I had ever loved, and had loved me.

It was then that I noticed, in the twilight, there it was; the beast that had been tracking me that previous night.
It was up near my daughter's bedroom.
No; I will not let anything happen to her!

I ran and jumped; even though I knew, it was not humanly possible; I managed to get onto the roof. There it was; ready to eat my child! I ran to it and grabbed it by the throat, the anger coursed through my veins and before I knew it, I was holding its neck and head, the body lay by my feet. I had become a monster. That is when I fled!

It was a while until I reached the wood that my uncle had told me to go too. When I reached it, I noticed that there were others nearby. They smelt like me, they moved like me. Those in front of me had torn clothing; dirt covered most of their faces. They were outcasts. Two of them approached me.
"Are you here to find yourself?" I heard one of them say.
I shrugged.
Then the one that spoke, took a dive off the edge of the cliff. Because he had gone so quickly it was like I was back in a plane ready to jump out. When I looked over the edge, it was as though someone had drilled a hole into the earth, just to see how deep they could go. The smell from the hole reeked of decay.
The second person, who had approached, gave me a push.

I was falling endlessly through the air wondering how far it was to the bottom.

Then something strange happened. It was as though I had new arms coming out of my back and attached to them was a thin clear skin; as though it was fine silk. My skin on my back tore open. What had once been gushing blood now stayed solid? I started to float down into the darkness.

Early morning and the sunlight beat through the thickest branches and yet it could not penetrate into the deep dank surroundings that I now lay. At the back of my throat the feeling of bile rose up and the food that lay in my stomach, including the wonderful steak, had begun its journey to freedom!

A group of rats crawled past me... something made me reach out with one dirt covered hand, I captured it. I knew now what it was that I hungered for; the urge was growing stronger and soon, I came over my repugnance to do it.

I sank my teeth deep into the creature; it was as though my teeth were now straws. Withdrawing the living blood from its body...
All that was left was a skeletonised skin of the rat.

*

So here I am, my clothes are covered in mud and dried blood. Sleep is not easy; my mind is filled with another's thoughts. The succulent taste of the coursing fresh blood as it reaches the throat, feeling it regenerate the body as though it were water. The thirst never goes it is only satiated for a time.

I'm surrounded by others; they're decaying as they starve themselves into absolution. It's like watching a cancer patient refuse meds, and slowly slip away as their body collapses in on itself. Wracked in pain and knowing they will soon slip from this world.

The rats come from the holes in the ground. I've noticed that they have started to fear me.

Light passes the top of the hole, it's the only way for me to mark the days that I have been here.

DAY 18

The bodies keep mounding. Only a handful, take flight, wanting to accept who they have become. I watch them in envy. Maybe I should just give into the lust! I can feel it growing; no matter how I try to divulge myself on the rodents that infest this hovel.

I saw something interesting today. One of my fellow wraiths that came in just the other day; waited for the sun rise. He winked at me and took off towards the sunlight above. To the dismay of others, his ashes floated down after only a few moments of his joyous escape. I could see the longing of the quick end from the others that were starving themselves.

DAY 21

So weak... so hungry... my mind racing... what if I was to try one of these corpses down here... would that work... Would that stop the hunger?
The skin taught on the bone... I opened my mouth as though to try and squeeze in, a quarter pounder; the teeth, needle fine, shredded straight through. I coughed and dust flew out of my mouth... well that didn't suck...

DAY ??

Maybe I should just do as the others. I have no strength to get up. Let alone fly like that lone crusader. What I wonder... should I have done it? The moment I saw the opportunity... No good now... I think I'll skip the next rat that comes along... Darn it... Ok that one just got to close for comfort... But it did feel good...
God why... just why... wasn't I good... why me..

The Second Coming

I lay in that pit for so long... I started to forget who I was. My mouth; constantly dry. My cravings just wouldn't quit. Soon I noticed that I was alone in the expanse. Surely the rats will stop coming now there is little for them to feed on.

I saw the sun rising above the crater. I am so tired. I wonder whether I can fly? I'm so weak.
I unfurled my strange apertures; I guess you could call them wings. If I can just find enough strength I can end this...

Finally I plucked up what energy I could, struggled to my feet. I looked up and was blinded!

Something else was floating down from the sun light, reflecting its rays somehow. No... the figure emanated light. It's wings were white; it's body clean and pure.

Finally it landed near me. I shielded my eyes from the light that shone from its irradiating presence.

"You... whom hath suffered. But hath not given up thou fight... I am Gabriel!"...

The voice didn't seem to come from the actual being. But instead it seemed to reverberate from the walls like a bass sound.

My mouth was so dry... in a rasping voice I responded.

"Aren't you... the messenger... of God?"

"Thou hast not forgotten. And nor hast our lord. I cannot tell you how he wept when he saw'eth your plight!"

"So why does... god weep for me..." my speech becoming more difficult as I could not produce any saliva to wet my throat with.

"He also had to give up his child... for your people..." There was a slight loathing in the echoes.

"Have I... not suffered enough? Can He not.... return me... to my family?" Anger began to pulsate from within. How dare he compare my suffering too his own?

"He hath sent me with this message..." The voice had turned curious as though wondering how to phrase it.

There was a long pause whilst the Gabriel deliberated.

"Our war... has now become yours... And He asketh of you. Which side do you choose?"

"What the hell are you talking about...?"

"I will forgive your blaspheme... he hath told me, to showeth you, the truth of the past."

The walls of the crater seemed to vanish. The darkness of the crater was changed to the darkness of the void of space.

"In the beginning son of man... We were his children. But soon he wanted more. He created this universe, followed by the stars and then the sun and moon. When the earth was created we thought it was to be a new home, for our kind. But then he created man. Thus began the first war. Brethren of wings; turned against each other.
Our lord stepped in cut the wings from the traitors. They fell to earth. Insubstantial and formless.

The second war however, was worse. Our lord let his own son get crucified by your kind, just to allow them the freedom of removing their sins. Something we were never given. The formless on Earth grew strength from the evils done by man and their influence spread to my former brothers...

Finally our lord, sick on the in-fighting amongst us and not celebrating his work. He burned those that rebelled and cast them out.
He had not realised, the strength the formless ones still possessed. For they gifted the outcasts, the ability to change man, into their own kind.
Conspiring with the Fallen, giving them purpose.
That sole purpose was to find those who would swell the ranks and create an army to take back Babylon..."

The images faded away and again the Angel Gabriel stood before me. His face a mask of placidity, but there was also a hint of sadness.

"So... Gabriel... What do you...? I mean what does God want from me...?"

"He wants you on his side...!" A gleam in Gabriel's eye surprised me.

"I can barely stand... talk... what good am I?" I could feel my energy dissipating as I slumped to the ground.

"He needs to know your answer..."

I looked up at the sky... before all of this. I never believed any of it would be true. Sure I went to Sunday school and read about the immaculate conception. The creation of earth and the stars... The rebirth...

"I will do his work... but in return I want my family protected..."

"It is agreed... "

The light vanished, as did Gabriel. Nothing was left but the hunger... Everything went black.

β

The Imam, The Rabbi and The Padre – The Rays of Light

The darkness was different when I awoke. I was lying on tarmac. I could feel the moisture seeping through my clothes from the soaked pavement.
I could hear cars moving, people talking and laughing, and music playing...
As I opened my eyes I saw the street lamps; orange glow reflecting from varying surfaces.

I struggled to find the energy to move.

I felt hands pulling at my armpits. They half picked and half dragged my lifeless body. My bare feet scraped up stairs and through a doorway. I was slumped down before some type of raised platform.

I heard words being spoken; however the language was unfamiliar to me.

A new voice in the darkness rang out.

"And what do we have here?" The voice thick with an American accent.

"We have... one of them... but something is err... wrong." The voice of another; thick with Jewish accent.

I felt water splashing down on me. Various things were being pressed onto me. From metallic to rough hewn wood. Words spoken in Hebrew, then Arabic and eventually the lord's prayer.

My hand was turned this way and that.

"Aha... Alpha and Omega... He has the blessing my brothers. That explains why this wraith, has been placed at our door. My eyelids were pulled apart.

"He has not fed..."

I saw a large man with a beard and a skull cap staring down at me through glass bottle spectacles. Around his neck he wore the six pointed saint David's star.

"Why would Mattatron bring us a wraith such as this... and leave the mark of God himself?"

Gradually I opened my eyes.

"Well brothers, perhaps we should ask him..?" The man with the cross around his neck and a beard that would make Santa Claus jealous, lifted my head.
In his hand was a goblet of pewter. Within it sat a dark red liquid. He lifted it to my lips and my teeth jutted out. I think they expected me to be something different.

I took the liquid into my mouth; strangely enough I could feel my mouth starting to salivate. Something it had not done for a long time...

"This my son is the blood of Christ..."

I heard the other two cough, as though they were in a dis-agreement with the words.

"Who are you...?" I looked at them in turn. The man in front of me spoke first.

"I am Father Meegan. But you can call me Padre."

"I am Imam Ali." His voice slightly more awkward.

"My name is Rabbi Levi. And you young man... Who might... you be?"

"I... I don't remember... The last thing I remember was an... no I'm..."

I didn't know whether to tell them of the visit of Gabriel. Or the visions that he had showed me of the battles within heaven. After all, it would have shot holes in all of their faiths...

The American Padre spoke again.

"There are stories young man... and I believe you are the first in a century to be brought to the head of the order of Ezekial... And since; by the sound of your accent. I think we should name you John.."

My throat felt better after the wine in the goblet.

"I'm sorry. Who? What ? Ezekial?"

This time the Rabbi spoke up. "Ezekial was the first of the three recognised faiths to have told us about the evils within this world, and beyond. He taught us to prepare. That is why we are here. Three... to show unity... against the true evils in this world!"

I sat up on my elbows and allowed my eyes to roam past the three men in front of me. I saw pews and crosses. The statue of Mary Magdalene, the idol of Christ on the cross.

"This is a church? Huh... how ironic... last time I was in a place like this I was..."

"Ah... that explains our informant... We heard from your uncle... he asked us to look out for you... and to try and help you!"

"How does my uncle... The smuggling...!"

"Why yes... young man he helps us to keep our brethren supplied around the world..." The padre smiled at me in that knowing way.

The others seemed to brighten up, almost relax in the knowledge of who I used to be.

The Rabbi and the Imam both looked at their watches simultaneously.

"I believe that you can handle this one Meegan... We shall check with you, come the morning..."

They bowed themselves out from the cloisters and headed for their homes.

"Can you stand John?" His voice was kind, like a grandfather speaking with their children's children.

As I got up I felt a pain course throughout my body, it was extreme. So much so, all I wanted to do was to fall back to the ground that I had come from. The Padre's hand clasped around my elbow. My wings dropped from behind me.

"I kinda forgot about these..."

He helped me from the stage and into an inner room. A fire blazed in the hearth, every time I looked at it I felt scared: The walls were covered in varying religious artefacts. He let me flump into the chair.

After; he moved over to an old oak writing table and pulled a bottle from under the shelves.

"I keep this for my own personal consumption... However since it was your uncle, who obtained it for me, I see that it only fit I share some with you."

He uncorked the bottle and the smell; rich with old fermented grapes; released its fragrance into the room.

"Why can't I look at the fire? I used to love looking at the fire, the way it licked around its fuel. Now it just seems to hurt my eyes and my mind..."

The Padre poured two glasses and came and sat between the fire and I.

"You were met by the Arch Angel Gabriel... Right? Well I'm sure he showed you how the Fallen were created!" He leaned in and handed me the glass.
"Well you must know that the fire in which the traitorous angels, were thrown throw... was none other than the fire of our sun."

"That explains an awful lot..." The wine touched my lips and strangely the hunger satiated again.

"That is why the sunlight cremates the Fallen. It's the same reason you can no longer stare at the fire. This is how we used to deal with your kind..." The Padre lent back and made himself comfortable in his chair.

"Ok... well how is it that my hunger is getting appeased by this wine? I had to drain countless rats and all I thought about was the sweet taste of the blood coursing through a living persons veins... I mean... All we have to do is get a load of wine and come to an agreement with those that turned me...?" I looked at him; I could feel my smile turning into a sarcastic grin.

"Ha-ha-ha if only... No the Fallen like those who turned you, are specific about who they take. God only knows why they chose you to be among their ranks. I guess they thought the moment you took your first bite, you would be there's..." The Padre smiled thinking of the idea.

"So how is it that this wine helps me? And why back when I was in the pit did I see the thoughts of the one that turned me?"
I could feel anger course through me thinking about the images that streamed through my mind. The feel of the fresh blood; the ecstasy of the first bite.

"You used to be a Christian boy. What does the wine signify at the mass?"

"Christ's blood?"

"Bingo... my boy you are learning... Now I see you have almost finished the wine in that goblet... Through the door over there, is the access to the crypt below. There's a few blankets and no light during the day... Tomorrow night we shall speak again and try to figure out what is to be done with you." He saluted me with his still half full glass.

I raised myself off the sofa. My limbs less achy, my body feeling a little more rejuvenated than it was before. This stuff sure did beat the rat delicatessen I had been dining on.

The door creaked open and the darkness crept from the top step down. I had to feel for a moment to make sure I didn't fall. Then, all of a sudden I started seeing in black and white. The shapes in the room became clearer as though I had stepped into an old black and white TV box.

*

The following night the padre opened the door and raised a candle so that he could see where I was. Unlike popular belief, I wasn't hanging upside down or stiff as a board in a coffin. I was just laying there sprawled in the blankets. The Padre threw down some clothes for me and then lit the candle at the top of the stairs.

I made my way up into his room: The fire felt like it wanted to leap out of the hearth at me.
A glass of wine waited for me.

"Please... sit. I have been talking with the others..." The padre paused as though he was chewing over the next sentence.

I picked up the glass and slumped into the chair. The wine was half way to my lips before I smelt something different.

"Have you blessed this..?" I raised the glass to the padre as though a simple wave of his hand would help out.

"I had hoped this wouldn't be so quick... Sorry John. We need you to go to somewhere else tonight... It should help you..." The Padre's face was grave as he swished the wine about in his own glass.

I stared into those green eyes wondering what he was thinking and then it struck me. The hunger... it would return with force; the same hunger that drove me crazy in the pit; the same hunger that got me to try and bite another Fallen! Could I go through all that again?

The padre had obviously seen by my expression, what I was thinking.

"There are other Fallen where we are taking you. Ones who have lived longer than any with the thirst pulling on them! We have other ways to save you that pain again..."

I placed the glass back on the small table near to the seat. As I went to stand up; I heard the screech of tires outside.

The Padre stopped me with his old wrinkled hand to my shoulder.
"You are now a servant of God. There is something I think you should have." He walked over to the fire place and reached around to the side of the chimney breast. It was long, wrapped in old cloth. "This was given to me from Imam Ali... It was an offering of trust when we first met."

Slowly he opened the wrappings. Within the depths of the old fabric I saw an ornate handle with a blade at both ends. The shaft was carved with Aramaic writing.

"What do these symbols mean?" He had handed it to me; it felt light, strong and fluid.

"They are in the original scribe of the bible. Basically it says... for god, his wrath goes with the bearer to vanquish the banished!"

I returned my eyes to his. He stared back at me, his eyes full of sorrow.

There was a knock at the door.

"It is time for you to go. Please use this wisely. I hope that we will meet again soon."

What else is out there?

The Padre ushered me out of the door with the weapon rewrapped and folded in my arms. A black BMW sat waiting; the tinted windows gave it the impression of a statesman's car.

I noticed the registration plates were different to the other cars in the street. It seemed as though; it were a different countries license plate, but it was not one I recognised.

A man in a dark suit and dark glasses stood waiting with the door ajar. Before I got in the Padre insisted on blessing me with a prayer of deliverance.

I thanked him for his kindness and slipped into the plush black leather interior.

I noticed after the door was closed that I could hardly see out of the windows. The back seat was comfortable and yet the view to the front seat was blocked by a large dark screen. I heard the driver's door slam closed, the engine purred into life. The car drove off like it was driven by a professional chauffer.

There was time I used to dream of being driven around in a car like this, now it, just seemed trivial.

It seemed like hours of staring out of highly tinted windows and seeing dim globes of streetlamps. I kept playing with my teeth. At the moment they seemed just like the ones I used to have.

The dark screen retracted slowly and I saw the driver's eyes in the rear view mirror.

"We should reach our destination before sun rise, sir... but just in case I might suggest that you..." He reached over to the seat, next to him and threw a black blanket back to me. "Get ready to throw this over you. The windows maybe tinted but at the sun up you could still be hurt. I know my people wouldn't want that."

"I'm sorry, this is very new to me. Your people? I still don't fully know what is going on..." I felt a pang in my chest as the hunger struck me. Crippling me, it was as though my joints where being attacked by a thousand stinging nettles.

"I have something that might help sir..."
The driver pulled open the glove box and pulled out a silver tanker.

As he passed it to me I could feel my eyes focus on his wrist. I could almost feel the rhythmical beat of his heart beating through his veins by his thumb.
The moment passed, I grabbed the flask. It looked like an old fashioned hip flask. The emblem on the flask matched the one that was emblazoned on the side of my hand. I opened the lid with a flick of my wrist and raised it to my mouth. It didn't smell like the usual wine that I was offered by the Padre. It made my mouth water as the smell wafted up my nasal passage.

"It's ok sir... it's just pig's blood... The closest you can get to having human blood."

I lifted it to my mouth and I felt my new teeth extend and catch on the bottle neck. The sensation was gratifying as I drew the thick liquid into my mouth.

"Thanks... So how is it that you got this... err... 'gig'?"

"Ha-ha yeah doesn't seem a great assignment does it. Well I got the call from a mate of mine. He said that someone like you... needed a lift. Well I'm between... 'gig's'... at the moment."
He smiled at me but I noticed something different. His teeth shone silver and looked like sharp canines. As he noticed me looking at the teeth; he removed his sunglasses and winked at me. His pupils, were slits.

"There's something different about you... What are you?"

"I'm surprised... Normally your kind, smell us first rather than see our differences... Sorry about the eyes, and teeth. It changes the moment we feel a dangerous presence, although it's usually those damn smelly dogs.."

I looked at him enquiringly. My mind was whirring, thinking back to the strange stories I used to read as a child.

"So you mean? Werewolves? There's more than one..?"

"Hell yeah: They're everywhere, the bloody smelly dogs." I saw he was holding a pendant with his gear shift hand that was around his neck.

"What's that?" I was getting curious about the chauffeur.

"It's the pendant of St Christopher. It was adopted by my people when the Christians arrived. It allowed us to blend in and not be persecuted by their kind!"

"Why would someone persecute you?"

"Ha ha you would say that now, we have so much cultural acceptance. But back in the Christians' darkest age, we were hunted as witch's beasts or thought to be your kind... Used to call you guys Vampires, that was until we found out where you truly came from.... Our old ways were not forgiven by the Christian faith back then."

"What do you mean 'old ways'? Do you mean Pagan?"

"Bingo. You guys call us Pagan where as we prefer to refer to ourselves as following *Fyrnsidu.* It means old custom... can I guess your next question...?" He paused for a moment to overtake someone.
"Every religion that has ever existed has brought with it, good and evil! Now people like you and me are here to clean up that mess..."

A jolt in the road made me spill some of the pig's blood down myself. As I looked up I saw a sign on the road illuminated; it showed that we were on the A1(M) and heading towards Nottingham forest.

"How far we gotta go...?" The clock on the dash read 2am.

"We still got some mileage to go... look I know it's frowned upon but do you mind if I smoke rather than stop... I mean... I'd rather get you up to our rendezvous before sun up. As you can guess, me smoking now means you don't have to worry about smoking later..."

The driver had already got his packet from of his jacket and was flicking a cigarette from its nest.

"Knock yourself out..." I sat back thinking of all the good things I'd saved myself for. "What's it like?"

The driver squinted back at me. "What? Where were going? Well it's..."

I cut in. "Sorry I meant smoking..."

"It's a filthy habit to be honest, but it sure beats the depression after seeing so many of my friends die..."

The driver seemed to go distant for a moment as he flicked the lighter into life, he drew deeply into the plant life in the stick. He grabbed the packet and threw it to the back seat next to me.

"Here... It's not like it going to kill either us..."

I picked up the packet, its emblazoned brand logo and golden box. The lid slid back to show the brown mottled filters and the white stem. I plucked one out and swapped his cigarette box for the lighter.
I put it into my mouth. 'In for a penny in for a pound' I heard my mind saying.

The lighter burst into fire and it took all of my concentration not to through it away at the first site. The flame danced closer to the tip as the end glowed a dark red.

The first full lung made me cripple into coughing my guts up. The driver opened the window beside me and I flung the cigarette out.
I finally got my coughing under control and apologised to him for wasting his cigarette. My mind raced from the nicotine and I felt myself passing out from the drug induced high.

When I awoke again it was to the call of the driver.

"Hey wake up fella... wake up..."

"I'm sorry. Never smoked before and I gotta tell you I don't think I'll be trying that one again..." My head was hazy as though I had to much sleep and I was trying to move about too much.

"Just glad I didn't give you a joint to be honest..." He said whilst puffing on another cigarette.
The clock on the dash was reading 4:30 am. The main roads had disappeared

and in the dim light I could see the hedgerows scraping the sides of the car.

"Gonna have to do your window up soon. We won't be long but if my memory serves me right, sun up won't be long and we still got a while till we get to the place..."

The window that I had quickly flung the cigarette was closing as well as the screen that separated me from the driver.
"*You ok in there... This is a private intercom.*"
The voice seemed slightly distorted.

"Yeah I'm ok... I think so..."

"*I'm glad. Now I'm sure we'll have plenty of time to talk later but now we gotta make sure we get through this last bit, without you getting a bad sun tan... Get that blanket on!*"

I could hear from the urgency in his voice that it was serious. I slid under the blanket and waited.

I felt the car dip down as though we were joining an intersection on a motorway. We then came to a full stop and I almost slipped straight off the seat. Thankfully I held the blanket for dear life.

Y

A choice

I remember being bustled for the car by rough hands. They zip tied my hands together, as though I was going to be a violent prisoner. The gift had been wrenched from my un-protesting hands. The blanket still covered me although it meant that at times I tripped over the unforeseen.
There were all different types of accents and languages being spoken, a lot of it I didn't understand.
I knew that we were underground because of the damp smell and the constant temperature.

I was physically thrown into a room, the blanket finally removed from my head. I saw the legs of my captors just before they left the room. I remember seeing black army issue boots and black trousers.

Another tannoyed voice called out.

"John... we are sorry for these measures. We have to make sure... you are not a risk."

As I sat up and looked around; the room seemed to be an old fallout bunker of sorts. The doors were fitted with spinning wheels and where rounded as though to prevent structural weaknesses should a catastrophic failure happen.

I shook my head until my eyesight steady again. The disorientation had affected me somewhat from the shoving and dragging.

"The heads of your order seemed pretty convinced... What's with the rough treatment?" My voice seemed raspy as though I could still feel that cigarette I had tried was stuck down my throat.

"John... we know what they said, but we gotta believe you too..."
The tannoy went to static for a moment.

'Great' I thought. 'Just when things were looking up and now I seem to be back in another bloody dark hole'.

The tannoy came back on.
"We got a series of tests for you to go through John... Just to make sure..."

The lights went off in the room. I felt like crying... They were going to subject me to this again. I felt myself rocking. That was until my eyesight kicked into black and white.

'DONG... ZZZ.ZZZ' The sound reminded me of the old strip lights firing back up. My eyesight impaired for a moment and then I saw them.

In two different corners of the room, there were two separate people. One of them looked like a creature similar to the ones I'd seen down in the pit... Well I guess my kind. The other, was a woman. Both of them seemed to be trussed up to some kind of pole by bindings of rope and similarly neither was wearing a lot...

Just enough to keep their modesty in check.

Another light came on not far from me; this time however, there sat a small stool were two items. A silver dagger and a splintered piece of wood.
I unfolded my wings feeling the exhilaration of the freedom I felt. I used them to pull myself to my feet.
There was something new. I smelt fear. Real fear, the kind people say that only highly developed hunters understand like sharks and such like. It tingled through me down to my toes. It's hard to explain, it's like that first shot of caffeine in the morning mixed with sexual orgasms.
I felt with my tongue that my teeth had extended and I looked towards the woman.
It happened again my eyesight honed right to her. I seemed to be impulsively scouring her body, seeing the sweat glisten, the skin smooth, supple. The veins around her neck pulsing. I followed that pulse with my eyes down towards her breasts to where I knew her heart

was pumping those wonderful sounds **'Dum-Dum'**... **'Dum-Dum'**..."
My eyes refocused. Something was on her chest. It was obvious someone had tried to cover it with makeup but for some reason I could see it... It was a tattoo... the shape was like large cat's paw...

She was like the driver.

I calmly walked over to the table and with both hands pulled the silver blade up to the plastic zip tie.

'Twap'

The tie was broken and fell to the floor. I felt my wrists trying to bring them back to life. I stared at the broken shaft of wood. Something about it, creeped me out. I put the blade down and looked again at the wood. It looked old. I placed my hand upon it and it thrummed in my hand.

I turned now with the shaft of wood in my hand and although I could still smell that unmistakable fear that was driving my senses crazy, for the delight of the pulsating blood, another feeling had come over me.

Was it pity? I looked at my own kind, it looked so sad to be tied up. I picked up the knife in my empty hand and walked over to the Fallen that had been strung up.

As I got closer I saw that this one had marks all over his body. As though he'd spent years being tortured!

I moved the knife up and cut the bonds that held it. Its face changed from sad to mad in a matter of seconds. You could say the smallest amount of time.

It pushed me away and lunged forward from its post. It had stopped at the far corner. I could see it eyeing up the woman. Her muffled pleas for help seemed to be heightening both of our senses. I longed for the sweet taste. Problem was... So did he!

Stalemate. The Fallen kept looking at me, then the woman, licking its lips and then looking back at me.

I wasn't sure if it was trying to say to me... 'Hey we can share this if you like... or... back off this one is mine and I'll kill you for it.'

It lunged toward the woman.
Even though it had a head start I felt that I had the upper hand. After all I've just eaten. The force of jump accelerated past the Fallen just at the last moment and without realising I had held the shaft of broken wood; blunt end on her belly so that the Fallen fell upon the pointed end.

I looked at her face. For some reason she was smiling, her eyes moved down towards her hands and I noticed a similar piece of wood was hovering about my sternum. I looked back to the fallen whom I had beaten to the mark. The face looked confused and then a moment later it was dissolving.

"Ashes to ashes... Dust to Dust... Fuck with me and you will also be... Mush..."

Her voice was but a whisper in my ear as I watched the sticky slimy remains of the fallen; fall to the floor.

I backed away from the woman. Her long brown hair and soft tan seemed strange against her green slitted eyes and silver teeth.

On purpose it seemed; she walked through the liquid remains of the Fallen that had fallen upon the pointy end of my stick.

She looked down to the stick. It seemed an odd thing to say.

"Shit's on your end of the stick... John"

With that she walked over to the door and men in black combats carrying assault rifles filed in.

The driver walked in

"Never did introduce myself properly now did I John... My names Logan..."

Who's who?

I was escorted away from the room by the armed men. Each one; I could feel there apprehension and pulses raised. Boy I must be scary.

They marched me into another room. This one was furnished by a large table and leather swivel chairs. Unmistakably a meeting room of sorts.
An old switch board to the side, showed a map. It seemed to be a worldwide map, with varying pins, the only difference were the colours. There seemed to be an awful lot of reds and greens and not a lot of blues.

I stopped in front of it for a while looking at our small island, sat aside from Europe.

"Don't stand on ceremony John... Take a seat."

Logan had somehow walked in without me noticing him. I turned and saw others were walking in. The last to enter was the girl who had been in my test room.

I sat down in the only empty seat and stared around at the different people who sat around the meeting table.

"I think an introduction should be in order don't you...!" Logan's hand shot out to the person nearest to him. It just so happened to be the woman with the green slit eyes.

She stood up with attitude.

"I'm Ma'beth Wolhawk..." She stared at me as though she wanted nothing more than to rip my head from my shoulders. Then with eyes still fixed took to her chair again.

"Next!"

"Werner... Werner Wolraven of the Nederlandse..."
He nodded curtly and sat back down.

The next person was a woman in pure white robes. The hood lay at the back of her head. She didn't bother to get up.
"Eselbeth... Of the Druidic order."
The girl next to her was intriguing, it was as though her movements were so flowing I wasn't sure when she stopped rising or falling from the chair.

"I am Rhoswen.. A representative of the house of Danu, the Faere."

"Sister Abigail... John." She almost bowed before sitting down.

The one next to her reminded me of the KP Crisps friars.
"I... am Brother...Simeon..."
He even had the look of one of the characters from the cartoon. You know Father who walks and does that corny line.

"Cap' Redman Sir... 4th Battalion. Rangers... on loan from the good ol' U-S of A. I command the garrison here."

I had to admit this one impressed me. It was the first American I had seen that didn't seem to be sitting with a bunch of medals weighing down his breast.

"Luke..." I stared over and saw another like me sitting just opposite. I could see he had the urges possibly worse than I had.

"Shin Tao..."

I couldn't quite fix my eyes on him; it was as though he wasn't really there.

I felt like I was back at school. I raised my hand in the air.

"John" Logan looked at me with a raised eyebrow.

"Logan... Sorry I can only smell four actual humans..." I pointed at each one. "And you guys..." I pointed towards Luke and the slitted eyed people.

"Sorry John... Shin Tao, here is a slight. We are very grateful for his ability to be here with us. Rhoswen there... well she comes from the old religions of our country." She nodded in our direction. "As for us..." He swept a hand around the ones I had named as 'guys'. "We are called the marked or Wolfsbane."

"Oh"
That's all I could think of to say.

Logan walked over to the board that I was studying as I walked in and started going through the situation. Apparently the blue pins were people like us. Not encouraging as there didn't seem to be many of us. The greens were known locations of Lycanthropic activity. As it turns out, it was to do with some bizarre curse back in the Arthurian period. The Reds were the Fallen activity.

'I gotta say by looking at that board I wondered how many normal people were left on this fair shore of ours'.

Logan flipped the board and it showed a much larger map of the UK and Ireland. This time at least there seemed a few more blue dots than the last one.

The meeting seemed to go on for ages and I felt my mind wandering between each person. My eyes kept automatically falling upon each one of their arteries in their necks. It was like my own personal dance music going off in my head.
Luke seemed to know what I was doing and once or twice, kicked me under the table.

Finally the meeting finished and I was quite proud of myself. I didn't lunge over that desk and plunge my straw like teeth into the first neck it came too.

Gradually we filed out of the room.

Luke's hand landed on my shoulder.
"I think we ought to talk you and I." I could see he had the DT's bad.

Logan walked past the two of us staring intently.

The guards; let us both go through into an access tunnel that lead to the surface.

"Here, we have a little time yet, before the sun rises again..."

I looked around; the shapes in black and white were beautiful... "Where are we?"

"Peak district... I know they tried to throw me off to... used to come up here when I was..."
He dipped his head down as though his memory pained him.

"I get it... when you were... normal right?" I put a hand on top of his shoulder.

"I don't suppose you have anything..." He held out his hand and I could see it was shaking bad.

Inside my wrappings the guards had left me, was the silver hip flask that Logan had left me before I left the meeting.
"its pigs blood and not a lot of it but here... I'm sure I can get more."

I saw Luke lift it to his mouth and force himself to down it as quickly as he could.

"I don't suppose you... made a kill... I mean a human...?"

"God no... Some Angel found me in a pit. Few innocent rats if that counts...?"

Luke started to sob out loud. His tears were rolling down his cheek with what looked like fresh blood.

"Hey man what's going on?" I pulled him into me. He wrapped his arms about me and I felt the warm tears moisten my clothes.

"I left them for him... and... and... he did this to me..." Luke seemed uncontrollable.

"I'm not sure I follow?"

"God told us not to love our own gender but I didn't listen..." His cries turned into sobs.

"You can't help who you fall in love with buddy... it's just one of those things... I'm sure he didn't turn you into one of these cause of that...!?"
He pushed away from me and wiped a tear from his face.

"You don't get it... it was my lover who turned me... The bastard had waited for me to turn whilst we lay in bed together. Then he took me back to my wife and kids in the pretence, to tell them it was over..."

He was looking me in the eyes. Shaking me, trying to get me to understand what he was saying.

"She started shouting at me... then I hit her... I saw her blood. I remember curling up into a ball because all I could think of was ripping her head off and drinking her warm salty blood. That's when he came in with that damned blade and the bloody goblet... It was already half full of blood. He shoved the blade right through her... I couldn't bear to see her like that so I tried to end it as quickly as I could. I let my teeth sink into her neck... all she could say was look after our kids..."

His eyes were black as night.

"The bastard had already killed my two kids and brought me there blood... I had drunk it before I realised where it come from... He was the first Fallen I'd killed..."

"What happened...?"

I looked at him in pure sympathy imagining if that had been me and my daughter. Anger pulsated through me toward the man who had done it to him.

I pulled him closer again as though wishing to remove his pain.

"The Angel came to me after I tried to kill myself in a church... He told me I could do recompense and see my family again if I joined there cause..."

He was still shaking but thankfully his breathing had calmed down.

He looked up at me. I think he had misjudged my caring for affection because he landed a kiss upon my lips. I pushed him away and I saw the lost soul in front of me.

"Sorry fella you just ain't my type..." I thought I should try and make him smile. "You ain't got blonde hair...!"

He laughed out loud and the awkwardness passed.

"What now...?" I asked him.

"Well they've got you... I don't want to be here no more... Damned if I've earned me place but I ain't caring no longer... I can't stand that feeling anymore. You know... like a ticking time bomb waiting to go off at a moment's notice..."

A cockerel crowed its morning warning.

"Look we need to get down below again buddy..."
I looked at him pleadingly.

"You go... I just want to look at that constellation again..." He pointed with a shaking finger up to the plough.

"You sure..." I levered myself from him and started my way to the porthole.
"Yeah go... I'll be with you shortly."

I climbed into the porthole and started my decent down the ladder. As I peeped over the top to see if he was following I noticed he had opened his wings to the full extent. The morning light was starting to spread over the horizon. I called to him.

"Luke... get you arse over here... it's time to go...!"

He turned to face me.

"John... it's your time now... good luck"

With that Luke began to glow red as paper within a fire. Embers spread across him like lightning.

I let go over the ladder and fell to the floor.

"

Then there was seven

The loss of Luke didn't seem to bother many of the people I had met in the evenings meeting. Apart from Rhoswen; she seemed to be deeply emotional about the fact he was gone.

In the days that followed Logan and Ma'beth spent time showing me how to fight with the weapon the Padre had given me.
Quite a few times I had nipped my own wings but thankfully the pigs blood that I was given helped me recover from the slight injuries I self inflicted.

"Our first assignment..." Logan stood in front of the table. It seemed strange that the chair sat empty.

Logan threw out the documents. Inside it showed various pictures of the capital.

"We have a... faction; who are trying to recruit near to Kensington..." Logan looked at me. "Your type of people John."

He winked at me with those slitted eyes.

"So far we've managed to figure out there mark... The girl in this picture is called Elizabeth. Not sure why she's being stalked but we've been asked by the powers that be... to step in. We got reconnaissance for the next few weeks... pack your shit we're off in ten."

Everyone got up and walked off; all apart from Logan and I.

"You sure I'm ready...?"

Logan smiled his silver smile. "Well if you ain't... we can always ask Brother Simeon to boot you up the arse!"

I laughed as he walked me from the room, his hand on my shoulder.

*

Elizabeth is on her way home... Tour De France has finished, the barriers are still up but the detour signs have gone. She doesn't know where she's going. So she gets out her phone...

Shadows from a doorway emerge, a group of five men. There leering at her... She's noticed and turns to walk anywhere but there...

*For every step she takes, they take two... Now begins the Wolf whistles and the '**are you lost love**?'*
Shaking with terror she takes the next turn.

She looks back as they menace the entranceway to the dead end street...
Hang on there's only four. She was sure there were five.
They close in on her...

Pushing and grabbing her screams heard by no one as the heckle of their laughter; sounds like hyenas on the hunt...

Her clothes roping her with every push and grab and grope...

Her mind racing... Hang on there's only three...

Two grab her arms and force her to the ground; her head hits hard on the concrete, her eyes blurring with tears... Can this really be happening...? Why is no one helping...?

Through the tears, pain and fear she sees something gleam in the night

The pressure releases from her arms and she curls into a ball...

More cries but this time it's not her... They are pitiful mercy pleading cries... Something wet cascades over her face... It's warm and salty to the taste... She opens her eyes... A hand is in front of her but something is wrong. It's limp and Lifeless...

She dares to look down... The forearm lay severed... Blood oozing onto the floor...

In the distance stands her savoir

She stands there; a silver blade at the throat of the owner of the severed arm, in the other hand something else... A goblet...

And now she is cutting back and catching the flowing blood in the cup...

Something is wrong... She is walking over; the blades tip dragging along the floor... Elizabeth crawls backwards against the cold wall...

She offers the goblet first... Elizabeth tries to squeeze harder into the wall...

The goblet is withdrawn as the sword is placed to her neck... she leans in and whispers "victims, aren't we all... "

*

I watched it from the roof tops. I was really impressed by the Fallen's swiftness. I could see the blood spray, the endless killing and feasting. That goblet; it reminded me of what Luke told me about his family. Maybe if he stayed with us, we could have found out together what it is about the goblet.

I jumped from the rooftop and spread my wings moments before landing. The blade of which the Padre had given me. Now named Saqit, held at the ready.

The Fallen stepped back. She watched my blade with interest.

"And what do you think you're going to do with that...young man"

She smirked at me, however, she carried on backing off.

Saqit twirled around my hands like cheer leaders baton; whirring through the night's air.

She nodded towards me as though accepting the challenge.
She raised her sword and parried off my initial strike.
"So where's the others... I can smell them..." She licked her long sensual teeth at me.

"They're ready... if I need them...!" For the first time I felt joy. Something about holding Saqit lightened my mood. It was as though the blades movements came from within me.

I moved Saqit around to my side and faked a lunge. She took the bait, lowering her sword to parry away my strike. I pulled the blade round and up so that the second blade whipped up and sliced cleanly through her wrist. The clatter of the sword echoed deeply in the empty street. I was so focused on seeing the hand fall I didn't notice her lunge forward; teeth and wings out to show. The goblet hit the floor. The pooling blood... seeped into the guttering.

In front of me the woman's face contorted into the hideous monster that fear brings out in the Fallen. She pushed me onto my back, Saqit held by her and I; like the constant pushing of the waves on the shore.

I heard a noise next to me. Out of the darkness I saw a catlike creature bounding across the paved floor. Its teeth bared, eyes fixated on the creature upon me.

With both paws it latched onto the wings of the Fallen on top of me and wrenched it off. I almost lost Saqit in the process. I jumped back to my feet in time to see a second Catlike creature attack the Fallen, which was pinning the head of the fallen with one gigantic paw. This one was a golden colour.

Out of the darkness I saw Brother Simeon; bible open and reading out loud "and the lord said to yee..."

A third cat creature was now dealing with the Fallen. Each one was holding either arm, head or leg.

Eselbeth walked forward out of the Darkness. She had the girl with her. The one the Fallen was hunting.

"Brother Simeon, what do you want done with this one?"
Out of the corner of my eye I saw a shimmer and there stood Rhoswen. Her eyes were glowing red. I realised it was her voice that I had heard but it was different to what I had heard in the meeting room. It seemed to echo like a voice in a swimming pool.

Brother Simeon took one look at her and signed the cross upon his chest.

"Take it back to the holding. Please... We must know what this Goblet. This is the first time we have seen a Fallen using this method!" He looked nervously at her as though she were a Daemon.

She glided more than she walked, her strange dress clung to her very body showing almost everything and yet nothing. In the dim light it looked as though she were wearing a tree. Leaves seemed to wrap around her. The rest was brown like bark.

She stared down at the creature that was pinned with the paws of the Marked. She placed her foot upon its chest and opened a bottle of water. Carefully she poured the water down so it cascaded around the body of the Fallen.
Just after she closed the lid I saw both the Fallen, and the others pinning it slide down into the pool of water.
I placed Saqit between my wings and turned to Eselbeth.

"What the..."

"The Faere can travel between worlds and between places using the earth's key resource... Water...!" Eselbeth said whilst holding Elizabeth close to her. Elizabeth herself seemed to be in a trance and had not noticed the bizarre occurrence that had just happened.

Shin Tao came from the shadows. "We have company..." He faded in and out of the world like a shadow passing between lights.

"I hate to ask this... as we are barely introduced but father Meegan said I could trust you... do you mind giving me a lift?" Brother Simeon pointed to the roof top that I had leapt from just ten minutes before.

My face lightened a smile. "How do feel about a hug?"

δ

The Goblet and the Blood

When Brother Simeon and I returned to the base; it was at least five hours later than the others. Logan met us at the underground bay.

"What took you so long..." his face full of glee and happiness.

Brother Simeon smiled at him oddly. It was almost envious but also loathing.
"You know my faith prevents me from excepting help, unless divine intervention allows me to trust **Her**"

I knew something was wrong by the tone of his voice.

"If it wasn't for my people you know the Faere would leave us to our fate... be grateful that Rhoswen is part Wolbear!" Logan's jovial expression didn't change.

Brother Simeon however, shied away from the continuing the conversation.

"Do we know anything about that goblet?"

Before I could say anything Ma'beth walked out of the shadowed doorway.
"She's not talking yet... The slag's full up. I'll need a few weeks before I can start on her." Her fists bulled up and the words came from clenched teeth.

"Thank you Ma'beth, may god bless us all with patience." Brother Simeon signed his chest again.

I looked from Logan to Ma'beth.
"You know... Luke mentioned about a goblet... when he was turned!"

Brother Simeon rushed to my arm. "He spoke to you? About his... turning?"

"Did he never tell you?" I was perplexed. It felt like they all held secrets from each other.

They all looked back at me shaking their heads as though oblivious of their former colleague's story.

Logan approached me. "I think we should talk..."

*

Logan had pulled me into a separate room away from the others. It looked like his own personal bed chamber.

"Pull up a seat John!" Logan sat heavily on his bunk and kicked off his boots.

"I know Luke's story and he bade me not tell anyone. Although I have to say he didn't mention the goblet you have just spoken about... I gotta know... Where does it fit in with his story?"

I run my hands through my continually growing hair and wiped my face with clammy hands.

"It's like this. The goblet seems to be an intimate thing the Fallen use. Luke was offered blood in it but after he was changed...?"

Logan started wagging his finger at me. "So far as we know the goblet is offered after the turning... but after this evenings events maybe it's not...!"

'*Knock, Knock!*'

"Come..." Logan looked at the door; meanwhile his hand had reached behind his back.

Brother Simeon and Sister Abigail entered the room.

"Blessings to you Logan. Brother Simeon has told me that John; here... spoke of knowing something of the goblet from Luke?"

Logan's hand came from the small of his back. In it laid his tobacco and papers. He deftly opened it one handed; whilst using the other to animatedly discuss the details; of the knowledge of the goblet. It was fascinating the way he could cover the truths he had spoken about in regards to Luke's turning. I was glad he mentioned nothing about his children and wife.

*

Werner knocked on my sleeping quarters.

"John. Come met me to the room. They have some understandings to explain to us."

I remember looking at Werner, even in black and white I could see his slitted eyes.

Werner stared until he saw I was up, then turned and walked off.

I pulled myself off my bunk and slipped on my trousers. Haphazardly I slipped on my shoes and on my way out grabbed a shirt.
As I walked on down the corridor I saw at each junction an armed patrol. I felt each

ones heart pounding the warm hot blood that flowed through their veins. I reached into my trousers and found no flask. I went to turn back but in front of me there was a shadow. Shin Tao came into corporeal form.

"John. I saw you leave this." He passed me the silver flask.

"Thanks, Shin." I went to turn away from him but a nagging thought came to mind.

"Shin... How is it you can... oh what's the right word... phase in and out."

Shin Tao placed a hand on my shoulder and started to lead me the way we needed to go.

"I am trapped. We have, not long for me to explain. But I remind you of this. You Fallen... Were not the first to be outcast! We are all in our faith trying to find redemption."

Something in my mind clicked back to Gabriel and the conversation of the first war.

Before I realised Shin Tao had practically walked me straight into the meeting room, whilst the others stared into the centre of the room.

The goblet gleamed in the centre. What was weird was that although it gleamed a kind of light it also seemed to want to focus your eyes on nothing else.

Shin Toa walked to the centre of the table and sent it flying.

The others woke as though from some terrible day dream.

"I hear many voices from this. It is not from this 'verse." Shin Tao called out.

Sister Abigail coughed and looked down at the book in her lap.

I looked over her shoulder. The page reference spoke of the cup of Christ. One of the greatest trivial mythologies in history; the cup of Christ, the Holy Grail, the immortalising cup.

This cup that now sat in the corner of the room looked nothing like it was described in the bible. This one was ordained with silver and jewels, inset with blood red rubies to red quartz. I noticed the inscriptions down the side were altering as I looked at them.

Shin Tao spoke again to the group.
"You must not look at this cup again. It is not from this world."

Rhoswen was the first to speak up from the terrible trance.
"Shin, thank you, the cups power reminds me of my Grandmothers own prowess."

Logan and Werner sat shaking their heads the way cats shake water from there fur. Brother Simeon was dancing his hands up and down and left and right.

"Shin, John... How is it that you can look at this without being affected?" Ma'beth asked.

I felt somehow I knew. My mind was going elsewhere. The face in my mind was as though I were looking at someone else in a mirror. It was the woman that turned me. She was whispering into the mirror but I couldn't quite hear her.

'**BANG**'

Shin had slapped the white flip board until it spun round and around.

"See here." He pointed at the shadows being cast by the board passing in and out of the light.
"It has come from here..." He then pointed to Rhoswen, Sister Abigail and then to Eselbeth. "And from you.. Your faiths!"

Sister Abigail was pipped to the post for disagreeing as Eselbeth rose to her feet. "My beliefs would never create anything like that, we believe in balance but this seems only to tip down."

"Shin... are you saying.. " Said Sister Abigail. "That this is a culmination of all of the dark entities in all of the faiths we follow around this table is where it come from.

Already shin had started to dissipate from view but he held enough power to shout "Yes and no...!" he then faded.

I looked about the room. They had started back talking to each other but I could see their eyes being drawn back to the goblet in the corner of the room.

Thankfully I had not put my shirt on. I walked over and threw the shirt over the goblet. It was like an instant snap.

"What just happened?" Logan was shaking his head again.

"Looks like you can't look at this without being entranced." I looked at the shirt, its colour distorting.

Sister Abigail looked at me then back down to her scriptures.
"If I'm right then this..." She pointed with the fullness of her hand. "Is an attempt of recreating the Holy Grail!"

"So why should this.. affect us all and not Shin?" Logan asked.

"I think I know the answer..." It was all clear in my head the reason that this being magnetised in their heads. It was because it was everything evil in their individual beliefs. "What's the most common issue we all have? Where there is good... There is almost certainly, evil...!"

*

They moved the goblet to the lowest part of the base that afternoon. Held within an old ammo box; marked with a satanic sign on the side.

The Fallen's Confession

Things start to change after the appearance of the goblet. For one thing my dreams were getting more vivid. I was seeing far more than I ever wanted to see of the woman who changed me, it was as though I was there. Here is how the dream went last night.

I'm in a room. It's large, but only has two doors that I can see. There are mirrors all around but I can't see any of the people that are within the room, the only thing I can see are the strobing lights pulsating to the music that seems to echo from the walls. I am looking around the room; varying people are bowing toward me as though I am a queen. I look down towards my wrist. The slender hands with black painted long finger nails glisten with the ultraviolet. The time piece is slight with no numbers just two hands. The hands tell me that it's coming close to eleven pm. I look up and stare over at the DJ stand. I can feel my hands rise over my head. Those around me stop dancing and like a bizarre Mexican wave everyone else stops dancing and looked straight toward me.

Their eyes were all black as night, one started yelling and I could see in each one, the teeth of the fallen.

The DJ began a new tune. It wasn't one I recognised but it seemed to be reaching a crescendo. All eyes turned to the far door as different men and women dressed in party clothes were pushed into the room. I could see tears on the cheeks but could feel little remorse as their hair was pulled back.

A voice spoke out within the room. A large black man in red thin sunglasses, adorned in robes fitting a catholic priest and yet they were dark red and the lapels were emblazoned in white skulls.

*"And he did cast us out... for his love of Man... he would forgive them but showed know forgiveness of us... therefore we rebel... we build... we **forge**..."*

From within his robes he produced the goblet that we had taken the previous night.

"He allowed his son to drinketh from such a cup... to adhere his mortality... we had to gift our immortality too personally... but now... we have been shown a way by the old ones..."

In the corner of my eye I saw slight's just like Shin Tao appearing from the mirrors. Only there forms were different. They were no longer in pure human form but seemed to stagger and crawl toward the huddled group.

"Those that will have drinketh from thine cup will become one of our number... and when there is enough of us... we shall return and wage the final war... and there we will toast to our victory!"

Five more of the priest figures walked forward with exactly the same goblets.

"These mortals shall have their chance to join us... or too fill the goblets for the others..."

One man tried to break away from the group, pushing and shoving his way through the crowd. The crowd themselves were laughing.

"It looks like we have a volunteer..."

One of the slights walked right into him. His body convulsed as though he were having an epileptic fit. When the convulsing stopped, I saw in his eyes a red glowing emanation and then he seemed to straighten his clothes as though getting ready for a meeting.

"This one shall be the first to turn... he has spirit that we need!" The taken body spoke deep as though it were from another realm.

Jerkily he walked back through the crowd. His head seemed to swivel through three hundred and sixty degrees looking into each one of the victims. Then his hand raised and pointed to one girl.

"She is pure!"

A priest stepped forward and withdrew a knife from his robes. It was strange; as it wasn't a normal knife, it seemed to be curved around his hand and went round in a crescent but the main blade was on the outside. It went to a tip. It was the tip that the priest was looking to; as others grabbed the girl and forced her up right.

The hair was yanked backwards and the throat bare. All that was around licked their lips as though staring at a succulent pig on a spit roast.

The knife's point was dragged across and her screams turned to gurgles as the windpipe began to fill with her own blood.

A priest came from behind and kicked the back of her knees as another filled the goblet with her pulsating blood. Her head and body looked like an old tankard. Pouring the blood; from her partially severed head into the goblet.

In turn each priest filled there goblet. The body was discarded to the floor and several of the fallen fell to the knees, lapping up the fresh blood from spilt on the floor.

The man with the slight within; grasped with both hands the goblet proffered to him and drunk deeply. The goblet was handed back and to my disbelief the slight simply walked back out of the body. Its form returning to the inhuman shape.

The man dropped to the floor, writhing in pain and agony.

When he stopped writhing I saw the change. Wings burst from his designer shirt. He stood, his eyes where the colour of the night.

In turn the varying victims were offered the goblet. Only one refused. She grabbed the knife from a priest and plunged it into one of the Fallen.

It merely laughed at her and pulled the knife in deeper, then grabbed her jaw and licked up her face. She screamed as other hands ripped her clothing from her. She started rising from the floor as the Fallen gathered around her. They had grabbed the arms and legs. Gradually lifting her up. She screamed and thrashed.

The feeling in the room was one of excitement. Each of the fallen that surrounded her; were now biting into any piece of flesh, drawing her living essence from her...

*

'KNOCK, KNOCK'

The hallway light crept in on me. At first it was blinding but it was only a moment. Sister Abigail stood at the door.
"I hope I'm not intruding..." She looked at me with pity in her eyes.
I threw the duvet across my lap as I sat up in my cot.

"What do I owe this pleasure, Sister?"

She walked over to the chair I hung my clothes from. Gingerly she sat on the seat.

"I can't quite get my mind off of the abomination of that goblet... Something... is wrong!"

I could see by her haunted look something had changed about her.

"You weren't always a sister were you?"

She picked up the cross that hung about her neck and stared at it.

"You are right. When I was young I was sold into the sex trade in china town. My younger years were not happy ones. Now I look to god for forgiveness to what I did...." Her voice soft but broken.

"That's hardly your fault sister. You can neither change what you did as I cannot change who I have become..."

She let the cross fall from her fingers.
"When I looked at that goblet I remembered the dark times. It was as though I longed for those times again. And yet I would never want to go back to

those days; as all I was to them was an implement for them to take their lurid sexual desires out. But..."

She stared at her hands.

"You long for that feeling within you... especially when you felt the touch of the goblet... Sister... I think I'm starting to understand. We need to gather the others..."

She seemed to snap out of the trance she was falling into, her hands where at her groin. She seemed shocked and wrenched her hands away.

"Of course..." She stood up and crossed her breast a number of times as though begging forgiveness from god to what she desired.

She walked from the room in a hurry.

I laid back on the bed and felt my manhood, raising the duvet. Her thoughts seemed to be flowing into my mind, like a residual movie plays on the mind.

I walked over to the chair and pulled the clothes on, then filled the basin and plunged my head into the soft water within. I didn't take my head out for some time.

*

The meeting room seemed filled with anticipation as I walked in. I sniffed the air and noticed someone else had joined us. A lady sat beside Logan. Her sultry dress; barely covering her shapely figure.
"Ah... John... this is Patricia..."
Logan began standing up and pointing to the lady.

"She's a Fallen..." I finished his speech.

"Yes..." Logan's eyes fell to his side.

"Welkom John." She stood up. Her long black hair falling down to the gape in her breasts.

I nodded towards her and took my place next to Shin Tao. His form seemed slightly different to usual, almost more. whole.

Sister Abigail stood up. "We have invited Patricia here from Holland to discuss the phenomenon of the goblet." She looked over at her but I could see her eyes were scanning her in a different way.
"Could you tell us what you know of this?"

Patricia stood once more. Her body enticing as she stood. She pulled from her body a long cigarette holder and placed a filtered cigarette to it before lighting it and taking a deep lung full of the smoke.

"I have heard of this from my latest girls. It seems the goblet is some new way that the fallen have found to recruit... The details are sketchy... but they have all turned up with black eyes!"

"What is the significance? I don't understand..." I looked at her. I could see she had black eyes.

She looked deeply into my eyes. "I see you have not..."

I couldn't believe what she was saying. Surely my eyes are like hers.

She could see the internal turmoil within my eyes.

"You have not taken a human life... you are still a white eye...!"

I felt gobsmacked. I suppose I wouldn't know as I can't even see my own reflection.
Shin Tao nodded to me to give me reassurance as to what she was saying, was true.

"You see the dark eye..." She pointed to her own eye ball. "Means that you have darkened your soul; by taking a life. I keep my girls that come in pure by gathering blood; for them, from willing clients. Some however take things a little too far... It's a good way for me to tell who has betrayed my trust."

Eselbeth spoke up. "So really why should we trust you...?"

Logan broke from his chair, snarling at Eselbeth. Patricia placed a hand upon him and she stared at him in such a way that he sat back down.
She then pulled her long sleeve up her arm and upon it sat the same mark that was upon my hand.

"I spent years upon this earth before I realised one day how far I had sunk... it was when she appeared..."

Sister Abigail raised an eyebrow to her... "Her?"

Brother Simeon leaned in, his pen and paper clicked and ready.

"The angel that appeared to me called herself, Aphrodite..." Patricia started.

Sister Abigail broke in. "The good book tells us that there are only male Angels and Aphrodite is a false god of the old religions..."

"I sister... am merely telling you what I was told! I was being given a chance to return the side of the saviours... After she visited me and showed me what I could do to return to the light. I embarked on a journey I shall never forget."

She placed her hand upon Logan's shoulder.

Rhoswen spoke up. "Perhaps you could elaborate on what happened?"

"For that I should take you back to my original life..."

I was born in the year 1876 I was nothing but a street urchin on the streets of

Dusseldorf; doing all I could to help my mother.

We lost my father to an accident in the steel works.

By the 1890's the ship works brought sailors from all over due to the ship building.

Where there are sailors there is work for a girl like me!

I earnt my pay on my back, on my knees or even on top depending what the different sailors fancied at the time.

After a while the word got out that I would do almost anything for the money and I have to be honest; the attention.

My mother passed away two years before the dock closed down due to more popular ports, drew away the business.

I knew that without the sailors I would be ostracised by my community. So I packed up my things and took the last ship to set sail.

I had saved enough to travel in third class and by 1906 I had found myself working my way through a number of

transatlantic ships, as a play thing for the rich.
I feel no shame, it was the only life I knew.

It was 1916; my fortieth birthday. I knew I would not be able to keep up the work I was doing and had stowed enough away to get me to the America's. That's when I found myself on the USS Kaiserin Auguste Victoria.
She was a beautiful ship. Steam powered, the ladies lounge was amazing.
It was there that I met the Count De Marque. Or should I say it's when I first met his wife. The Countess De Marque.
She was a beautiful woman. She caught my eye whilst she sat sipping on her glass of Vodka.

Her eyes were strange; I thought at the beginning that maybe they were some kind of genetic default. She always wore coloured spectacles but I noticed them when she tipped her glasses at me. One of her ladies in waiting came into my humble bedchambers later that night. I didn't realise but that it was to be the night was changed.

The night was rough. The boat rocked so hard that walking was like being drunk.
The lady seemed to be upright; no matter how rough, the sea got.
She didn't really speak but rather offered her hand towards me. Her eyes were pure white. I thought that maybe she were blind because of it, but now I know different.

She led me through the ship to the upper quarters; passed the ships sailors who seemed to simply see past the lady in waiting and I.
The halls became more elaborate as I stumbled along the corridors. I don't know why I followed this lady I just had a sense that there was something worthwhile in it for me.
Finally we reached an ornate door made of mahogany; the plate on it said Captains Quarters.

She knocked on the door and it opened into some type of party.
There was a violin playing in the corner of the room. The Countess approached me the moment I walked in. The lady in waiting seemed to blend into the surroundings.

The countess stroked my cheek and allowed her hand to fall down my neck, between my breasts and down to my naval.
The touch sent shivers throughout my body that I cannot fully explain.
I felt hot and flustered just from that one touch. She took my hand in hers and pulled me forward; toward the centre of the room.
"Zis is the Woman I told you about my Count..."

The count himself was so very handsome. His high cheekbones and square chin reminded me of a one that was of a highborn noble. He too wore glasses that were tinted in colour.

He picked up my hand and pulled it towards himself. At the same time; bowing so that his long flowing hair brushed my hand at the same time. It was like another jolt of electricity ran again through my body.

"I have heard you are a Courtesan of high regard Mademoiselle, we are honoured to have you with us..."

I could feel myself blushing. To be called a Mademoiselle at my age was a compliment. He took my hand and pulled me into the centre of room and began to dance me around to the music that was playing. With each twist and turn I felt his body rub up and down me with sensuous movement.
The music changed and the countess joined us within the dance. I felt her hands stroking my body with the rhythm of the music.
As we danced around the room I felt my clothes slipping from my body as though they had been snipped from the seams. My hair was undone and fell about me.

The count lent in on my shoulder and began to kiss the countess. I could feel the hot breath about my neck. The warmth of their body against mine as they rubbed around; feeling my curves, my breasts. The countess pulled me by my hips to face her. As I looked down I noticed that her clothes were also gone from her body. Her slim shape and small breasts rubbed against mine. She pulled me closer and began to kiss me upon my lips. The taste of her mouth; smooth and tender. It was not the first time that I had been kissed by another woman, but this was different, this gave me a different sensation through my body. As though I was being tormented, as I used to torment those wishing to pay for my services.

She stroked my body and reached down to between my legs. Her hands pushing apart my thighs. The count rubbed his naked body against mine and I felt him pressing on my buttocks. They both went either side of my neck and that when I felt the first bites of my life. It was exotic and sensual, my body shivering.

When I awoke the next morning the lights in the cabin were out and I could feel the naked bodies of the count and countess on either side of me.

I slithered out from between them and picked up my ruined clothing from the floor from where they sat.

I had started making my way to the door knowing that this type of people sent payment via there ladies in waiting. I passed a mirror but paid no heed to it. I was sure that the mirror would only pass judgement, on my aging skin.

I hurried through the corridors and heard a few wolf whistles from the sailors that saw me pass. I was sure I would have more work from them later but for now I needed to be dressed again to prevent the talk of the other passengers on the third level.

I quickly opened the door and closed it behind me thinking of the things that had happened whilst I was within the Captains Quarters. I felt my neck and felt the puncture marks on either side. I went to the small mirror in the room and tried to look at how bad my hair looked. That's when I freaked out!

My reflection was not there. I went over to the small washbasin and jug. I poured it and splashed the water in my eyes. I went back to the mirror and to my dismay my reflection was still not there.

I had been lucky to be blessed with a porthole. Something that many in the third class section would never have had, if I hadn't slept with the quarter master.
I slipped the cover open and the bright sunlight burnt as it hit my face.
I screamed and the lid slid back over the light.
I rolled on the floor; it felt that my face had been splashed with hot oil. I splashed my face with the water that was still in the basin.
I guess a sailor must have been passing my door when he heard the scream.

He burst into the room, looking around for an assailant.
He must have been just a boy of nineteen.
"You ok miss? I heard you scream... Oh... I'm sorry miss I had no idea you were..." His voice dropped away as he turned and closed the door. He remained in the room though.
I was still naked and my body was yearning for something.
"It's ok young man. I'm sorry I thought I saw a rat..."

He jumped right into my body. My breasts hot against his hands.

He was so bashful, so full of life... so delicious.
I placed my hands about him and pulled him closer. My eyes narrowed to his neck, the pulsating vein going to the rhythm of the music I had heard the previous night.
I knocked the hat off of his head. As it hit the floor he looked down to the floor. I opened my mouth and bit into the vein.

The sensation as I withdrew the blood into me was exhilarating.

Eventually his drained body slumped to the floor. That's when my wings first appeared knocking the ornaments from the wall, in a din.

I wiped blood from my lips. The sensation was like nothing I had ever felt. It was better than any real orgasm any man or woman had ever given me.

I shuffled his body under my cot and found a dress and shoal that would cover my new found apertures. I left the room with my meagre belongings and wealth. It was as though they knew because as I walked from the room; a lady in waiting to the countess, stood waiting for me.

She took my hand and led me back to the room.
This is when I first saw the goblet. It sat on a peddle stool and by the side of it sat a strange sword in a black scabbard.

The count and countess welcomed me back to their quarters and for the duration of the journey back to Europe I spent long nights and days wrapped in pleasure and eroticism. I had brushed off the incident in the lower levels as though it was nothing other than a bad dream.

The First World War was spent in a castle in Switzerland. The castle was up in the Alps, hidden away from the rest of the world.

The countess had people coming in constantly like sheep. Giving their blood to sustain without turning them into us...

I noticed that the ladies in waiting all still had white eyes.

I asked the countess one day and she explained that the blood given voluntarily and not taken by force would retain the innocence of the Fallen.

In the year 1937 the count and countess took us back to Prussia. What is now called Germany. They said that they were returning for the bounty.

When we got back to the city I saw pictures of a man with a moustache. He held his hand up as though wanting to ask a question.

Strange men started turning up at the mansion that we stayed at. At first there were German soldiers. The count and countess offered them my services and the countess herself watched over me to make sure I didn't turn any. Then there were others. They smelled like tramps mixed with wet dogs. It was later that I found out that these men were the Lycanthropes.

A year passed as the mansion turned into nothing more than a brothel. The ladies in waiting and I were the prostitutes.

Something clicked in my head one day when I realised that I was being used and not being paid for it.

Under the cover of darkness I left from the servant's entrance. Something was changing within me. I wasn't sure if it were a consciousness creeping into me or whether it where a fear for my own life.

I made my way to Bavaria; the money I had stowed for a rainy day came to my aid as I tried to put as much distance from the Count and Countess.

By 1939 I had found a small village in a town called Zwiesel. The people were nice and a couple offered me sanctuary during the day.
I didn't realise then that would be one of the staging areas of Hitler, Wolf Wache. The Werewolves had aligned themselves with the Fallen and Hitler. It seems he was hopeful to use their powers to gain the upper hand in World War 2. I think they thought that the persecution of the Jewish people and the Romany Gypsies would extinguish the hope that the allies would prevail.
This is when I met the first Wolfsbane and Faere Folk.

Their names were Pasquaile and Rose.

Deep within a forest I followed the Wolf Wache. They didn't march, they ambled. Sniffing the air. They only hunted on the full moon. There transformation was nothing but disgusting to watch. Ever seen road kill happen in front of you? Well that will give you an idea.

I saw from above the devastation of a horde of werewolves can do to the marked ones.

The only ones who were left alive were the Faere and the witch.
The Faere was badly hurt when I landed, the witch grabbed me using the cold limbs of the trees.

The witch took me back to the Netherlands with her.
She showed me a different world. One that I could be of use; not just on my back.
It seemed that I had become a Florence Nightingale for the Polish, American and English troops that landed in 1944. I saved some hundred lives by taking

lives. The German soldiers feared the one on wings.
It didn't matter whose blood fed me, it just mattered that I was doing something other than servicing those of the third Reich.

In 1945 the last of the Germans were routed from the Netherlands.
I walked into the remains of the St Peter Canisius. Only a part of the church remained. I hadn't been to church since I was a little girl and then that was to bury my father.
Cheers of revelation were sung outside of the debris. Freedom had come for the allies. I approached the Chancel. That of which was still standing...

The cross still stood on the wall. I sat down in front of it and I don't know why. I just started crying. That is when she came.

The angel appeared and offered me a different life. One that would help me; save others the pain I went through.

Patricia finished her story and we all looked about at one another. I could see Captain Redman staring longingly at the way she moved.
However Brother Simeon was heavily scribbling down each detail that Patricia had spoken.

I stared around the room.

"You know... I have something to tell you regarding these goblets..." I said my voice seemingly meek as I tried not to let my eyes rest upon Patricia's breasts.

ε

Common first bites

The story Patricia told and the way she described the countess was vaguely familiar. Those around the table were still in awe of the story that Patricia had just spoken about.

Sister Abigail straightened her dress and let go of the cross she was holding. She seemed flushed by the story.

"The Erm... goblets... you mean there are more of them John?" Her voice shaky

Shin Tao placed a hand on mine. "He speaks true. There are more than the one we have captured. The first constructed these goblets. Six all told, six created by six of my kind taking six days to create!"

I looked toward the slight's form.

"How do you know?"

"I, to my shame was one of the six creators of the goblets... I was lead to believe they never made it to this realm...

Only humans could have found a way to bring them into this realm." Shin's voice trembling.

"I had a dream about six goblets and six priests in red robes. The woman..." I looked towards to the alluring form of Patricia. "I think we were turned by the same person."

Patricia's wings burst out and her teeth grew. "Impossible... I was told she was ended by Luke the last of your Fallen warriors..." She slumped down into her seat. Logan passed his hand over her shoulder and pulled her into him. Softly she said "Impossible..."

"I know what I saw. She was in a small room with..."

Patricia finished my sentence for me.

"A night club, strobing lights..." Her voice trembled. "I thought it was just a residual memory from one of my previous... bites..."

"Last night... the image showed six priests and six goblets being used to change others..."

Eselbeth was the first to speak up. "Does that mean we have one of the six or have more been made?"

"No more will have been made. For it will contaminate the others. A strong will holds them together." Shin was starting to fade again. "I cannot hold myself here longer, I must go back. I will make sure that what is being told is true and that they are here..."

With that his hand and form disappeared from the room.
The Captain spoke up. "How can we trust this...? Slight?"

Brother Simeon spoke up. "We have every trust in Shin. God has given him his word that once the Fallen and the First are stopped he will have his place back in Heaven..."

Patricia scoffed at his statement. "Who said God is a He?"

The humans around the table jumped up to argue the comment. The others merely sat back in there chairs watching the argument of sexual orientation.

Werner got up from his chair and walked calmly over to the blackboard. His nails sprung out and he pulled them across the board.

'Scree...'

"Once we have stopped arguing... there is a bigger problem than an ethical debate... we must find these... goblets..." His eyes stared each one down with a cat like stare.

Ma'beth stood up and stood by Werner. "More Fallen will mean that the enemy will have a greater chance of starting their holy war all over again!"

Patricia stood up in front of the table shrugging off Logan's trailing arm. He looked longingly at her.
"Need I remind those at this table that our common enemy almost managed to recruit enough during the last world war. If it weren't for your predecessors then this world would be the staging ground."

Sister Abigail bowed her head. "I remember well the lessons I have learnt from Rabbi Levi..."

"So you know that he and his fellow's were rescued by the order just before they were to be changed. **Not all of the chambers were gas chambers**..."
Patricia's last words whipped out from her mouth like the crack of a horse whip.

"If I remember well it was Luke who saved the Rabbi... as well as many others." Sister Abigail's voice was calm but hollow as though she were ashamed.

Patricia's voice seemed shaky. "Luke... was a savoir to many..."

I couldn't help myself. "You said Luke said he killed this... countess. The same one, if I'm right that turned me!"

"He told me himself that he had killed her. But I wonder if he did or whether she wanted him to believe he had killed her... she who had her own husband turn him..." Said Patricia

Things were starting to fall into place in my mind. I realised that it seemed that the pair were something more than the usual turned.

"Patricia... the count and countess you mentioned. Do you know if they were once turned?" I looked into those black eyes.

It was Eselbeth who spoke. "I believe the pair you are speaking about are some of the original fallen..."

Brother Simeon stopped scribbling. "The Original Fallen?" We thought they were wiped out in the great purge.

"Oh yes my people remember about the great purge. Your people considered anyone who was not of your religion a threat. That is why there are so few of my people left. Be grateful that we are still here..."

Brother Simeon dropped his head.

"This in-fighting will not help us... what is done is done. I suggest we talk to each of our contacts and find the goblets first... then we can carry on pointing fingers!" Rhoswen stood up and walked out.

"Well I guess this meeting is adjourned." The Captain stood up and nodded to those around the table.

Gradually the others filed out. Logan stood talking with Patricia. The sister and I sat watching them.

Logan kissed Patricia's hand and bid us a good rest.
Patricia turned to the pair of us. Sister Abigail seemed different whilst looking at the shapely figure of Patricia.
"Should I leave you two too it?" I felt somewhat a third party.

Patricia walked smoothly up to both the sister and I.
"I think we should all stay..."
She looked me up and down as though sizing me up.

She placed a hand on both Sister Abigail's head and mine. She closed her eyes and soon a I felt my eyes begin to close.

When I opened my eyes again I could see a strange room. There was a violin playing in the corner of the room. A large bed dominated the room.

"Come; take a drink with me..." Patricia's voice was silky and smooth. Both I and the sister were standing within the room.

I felt the room sway as though we were at sea.

"I thought that this would be a good place for us... to get to know each other... we are after all.. Gods children!"

Sister Abigail seemed different somehow. Patricia walked up to the Sister and began to stroke her face. Gradually pulling the sister closer; their lips touching, their hands enclosing on each others, with tentative touches. Gradually Patricia began to loosen the clothing of the sister and although I wanted to look away I felt as though I couldn't. Patricia turned her head towards mine.

"There is a reason we were banished from Eden. At least the Sister agrees."

She seemed to know what I was thinking. Especially as the sister was also beginning to slip the dress from Patricia's seemingly ageless body.

Gradually I managed to release the image of the two ladies in front of me and look around the room. This looked exactly like the room that Patricia mentioned in regards to her initial turning.

The goblet sat on a stone pedestal to the side of the room. The symbols upon it looked strange. Out of place!

Two hands grasped hold of mine and pulled me towards the bed. It was only then did I notice I was undressed.

Hidden Truths

I woke up within my cot. The room was quiet but I could smell fresh blood. I knew it wasn't my normal pig's blood. I felt my lips and felt a dry flaking substance fall off. I felt alarmed that I could have possibly taken someone's blood against their will. I rolled out of my cot and went over to the shaving mirror that was within every room in the base.

I sat there trying to look into the mirror feeling stupid that I had forgotten I can't see myself.

A noise from behind me made me look away at the non appearance of my reflection.

Patricia rose from the blankets that lay strewn on the floor. I could see her in black and white. Her naked body; luscious and arousing.

She smiled at me as though I would remember what had happened the previous night.

"What happened?"

"Ha you don't remember... you were quite the participant..." She licked her lips and I saw the dark flaking blood fall from her lips.

"Who's blood?" I shivered when I thought about the blood on my lips.

Another person moved within the room.

"Sister...?"
The sister groped blindly in the dark for some clothing to throw about herself.

"John... Erm... I'm sorry..."

Patricia walked up to her and stroked her bosoms. "You didn't complain last night Sister."

She almost jumped out of the sheets she was covering herself with.

"Oh don't play coy with me sister... I know you remember last night!"

Frantically the sister felt her body as though expecting to find puncture marks.

"You won't find any because I would not turn anyone... it would jeopardise my agreement!" Patricia's smile beamed in the binary colour.

I walked over to the sister and passed her, her clothes that she wore the previous night.
"It's me sister... I cannot remember anything..."
She nodded blindly towards my voice and began to dress under the covers.

I helped the sister to the door and turned back. Patricia was against me. Her full naked body pressing up against me.

"I thought Angels. Even Fallen ones are supposed to be without gender.."

"Don't be so naive John. Who do you think Adam and Eve learnt it from? Free love is probably the only gift that God herself gave us..." She licked my cheek and then stroked down around my manhood.

I don't know why I felt so awkward but I could not help the feeling of being violated. I pushed past her and grabbed my clothes on the chair.

"I have to speak with Shin. The image I remember from last night. The pedestal that the goblet sat on had significance!"

"I did notice you weren't paying me attention John." She had crept up behind me.

'Thwack'...

She hit my bare behind so hard that it felt like the hand was still there.
"Don't fancy it again then?"

I shuffled myself away from her feeling hands and left.

*

Logan found me. I had been wandering the endless corridors looking for the right room but so far I found nothing but troop quarters.

"John... have you seen Patricia or Sister Abigail?" His voice seemed urgent and worried.

"There... there both fine Logan. I saw them both just five minutes ago." I thought to myself 'in fact I have seen more than I feel I should have'.

He breathed a sigh of relief and then looked at my dishevelled look.
"I see Patricia spent the night with you then..."
His face changed to a cheeky grin. "Got to love the dexterity of that woman!"

"Erm... look, Logan. Whatever happened last night I don't remember much but something I do remember is that I saw a goblet in my dreams again." I wasn't sure if it was my dreams or Patricia's.

I stopped one of the passing patrols and asked for a pen and paper.

Drawing carefully I showed him some of the symbols that were upon the pedestal that held the goblet.

Logan stood deliberating over the symbols with his hand on his chin.
"Have you showed this to anyone else?"

"Only you… I wanted to know what Shin thought of this!"

Logan carried on stroking his chin.

"There is someone else we should speak to first…!"

Logan took the pad and walked away still studying the symbols I had sketched.

The route took us down lower into the complex. I could feel the density of the air.

Finally we stopped in front of a big metal door. On the front of it almost burned into the metal was one of the symbols from the pad.

"What does it mean?" I said pointing to the scorched marking.

"The hell if I know. You gotta remember John we don't all follow the same religious strain as each other... You've been caught in one war as I'm caught in another... but we're all fighting the common enemy"

The wheel span and the locks released. It was as though the door was a seal to freezer as smoked hissed from the seams.
There was a blast of noise within and the light from within was blinding.

"Oh I forgot... put these on!" Logan was already wearing dark glasses and ear protectors.

The dark glasses seemed to alter my eyesight to the usual binary vision. Mostly the room was white however various symbols sat on the wall from the St David's star and the Cross, along with scrolls that could have been written in

Chinese and I swear a wooden totem that looked like it was adorned with skulls five pointed stars.

Logan plugged something into the ear protectors I was wearing.

"Can you hear me john?"
Logan seemed to scream at me but all I heard was a faint voice.

I held my thumb up to show him I could hear.

Logan pointed with his finger towards the centre of the room. Held up by chains was a figure of a fallen. It looked emaciated and drawn. The smell was repugnant and reminded me of the days and nights I watched the other fallen in the pit of which I started my new life.

"This is the count... count De Marquee..."

Realisation dawned upon me. His features although drawn were exactly as

Patricia spoke about. His shackles held fast.

"Luke could not bring himself to kill his former lover. Therefore we brought him here just after the last war… If it wasn't for the Imam we would never have finished his binding from preventing him from pulling his disciples to us."

Logan walked up to the limp body of the count. His hand outstretched. The pad of paper; displaying the symbols. The count hardly moved but I could see his black eyes looking towards me.
Logan reached up and slapped the count hard in the face. Then pointed toward the paper.

"Is this your symbol?"

I moved round to Logan's side and looked at the piece of paper. It was the same symbol that was burned into the door.

The count merely looked again at me. I could feel a weak presence trying to crawl into my mind.

Logan looked at me but I could feel my mind being dragged towards his.

"What's he saying?" Logan shouted into the room.

My mind slowly spinning and I began to see an image forming in my head.

The land was bare. It showed nature at its fullest. Night had fallen and the crickets chirped the evening song. The eyes I looked through focused upon a hill toward an old turret shaped castle. Smoke rose from the top and chanting could be heard echoing from the top most part of the castle. I felt my body lift from the floor as the image flew me to the battlements above.
Standing upon the battlements in front of a fire stood a woman. Her hair black as night and clothing of medieval finery.

"Morgana Eselbern…"
She looked at me in such a way that I felt awkward,

"My dearest Fallen warrior. Your timing is impeccable…" She walked around the fire looking at it and then back to me as though daring me to come closer to it.

"I am no fool Morgana… you have sought me out and now I wish to know why?"

Morgana twirled a single flame around her finger as though it were a toy.
"I want what you want Fallen. I want this land… and I'm willing to share it with your kind…"

Slowly I walked around the shadows cast by the fire, moving away from morgana. I knew she was not party to the same rules as mortals are. She followed a different mistress.

"You know that your own Father has aligned himself with the Order of Ezekial

and has convinced Arthur to join in his crusading… I'm curious… why should I align with you?"

The mention of her father seemed to shoot the very fire into her eyes. She was so easily taunted. If only she could be converted to the religion from the east then I could take her and she would be magnificent.

"In three months time I shall have an unstoppable army that the order will not see coming. Join me and I will make you my commander…"

I turned my back for a moment as to show contempt for her proposal.
"If I joined you Morgana, would you renounce your old ways after we won and join forces with me?" I turned to look at her. She was walking through the flames as though they were not there.

"See Fallen. I need not fear the elements in this world as you do. My Goddess grants unto me the powers you may never have. Why should I lose that gift?"

I looked full on into her eyes. I could see the fire she held within them. She did not intend to share; neither did she intend to allow us to remain.
"Let us see this almighty army of yours, Morgana… then we will see what you bring to the table."

She seemed to writhe in the fire as though it were drawn to her like she were dry kindling. She raised her hand, fist closed and red hot. Gradually she opened the fingers and within sat a rune stone.

"This is a gift from my mistress to your kind. It will help you in the days to come." She dropped the rune stone to the floor. I reached down to grasp it and although the main of the stone was cold as I turned it over I saw a symbol sat upon it. It glowed read and began to burn through into my hand. The stone itself disintegrated.

Morgana had turned to walk through the fire again.
Her words soft, as she said. "The first step in retrieving the immortal goblets; forged by the six, in six days, for six goblets... The key is to find the other five symbols."

The vision disintegrated in front of my eyes...

ζ

One of Six

The experience had made me fall to my knees. Logan grabbed me by the shoulders and pulled me out of the room.

He splashed me with water and sat in anticipation.

"Logan..." I croaked as though I had a lump in my throat that wouldn't go.

"It's ok lad... first time I went in there I fell to my knees... in fact the only one who hasn't is Shin... good point actually where is he...?"

A voice came from behind us. "You should have waited Logan. I knew John was not ready..."

I muttered. "One of Six... Morgana..."

I felt both of their eyes falling upon me. Logan's hand rested on one shoulder and Shin's slight corporeal hand rested on the other.

"Morgana… Eselbern… She was the one that gifted the first symbol, from her Goddess…" I felt like I was having an asthma attack. I just couldn't get my lungs to breathe out.

"The further away you are the better you feel, my friend: Logan come let's get him away to the upper floors…"

Together they helped me to my feet and led me to a lift shaft that I never knew.
The grating noise of the mechanics made it sound as though it was rarely used.

"Don't worry… this old thing is still good lad. We'll get you top side and into some nice fresh air."

The doors squeaked open; the smell of neglect on the rusting pulleys and cables dominated the small room.

Logan bashed one of the buttons and almost had to force the door shut with his own strength. Meanwhile Shin squatted by me.
"Logan. What brought you too the room?"

Logan produced the notebook from his pocket. "This…!"

A long low hiss emanated from Shin.
"I know how they got the first one through the veil…"

It was as though they had forgotten I was even there.

"This symbol has something to do with Morgana…" Logan started.

Shin continued as though he knew part of the story.
"Morgana walked through the fire and gifted the Fallen a token from Mab. The first key for the first goblet…"

"I know the girl was evil by why align with a race that would rather convert you than fight by you?"
Logan's voice was a wonder.

"You know the Wolfsbane origin Logan. Merlin had to find a power greater than what he had already just to perform that gift."

"What are you saying Shin? Merlin sided with the enemy to defeat Morgana. Surely the Fallen have no power of that type in this realm. Only that of turning…"

"There is a lot you don't know about my freedom from my kin."

Logan's voice grew stronger as though he didn't want to hear what Shin was about to say. "Merlin was always on the side of the good Shin. You can't convince me otherwise!"

"Merlin needed help. Even the all the Druid's all the seers and all the mages in the world would not have come up with the mark in such a short time. The old ones bargained for the power…"

"So you mean to tell me that the Mark… is some sort of high-breed of multi-faiths…?"
"Logan. I was one of the creators of the six goblets. Although we made them we knew not the keys to get them into the world… It seems that Mab did."

"The old tales always said about Mab resurrecting her subjects. Do you mean she knew about the keys…?"

Shin shook his head. "Mab knew of one key which she revelled in using time and again to the frustration of the old ones. You cannot imagine how many variations of hell there are and the tormentors hated her for taking away the ones she wanted back."

"So…" Logan breathed heavily as though the thought of the puzzle starting to form an outline that would mean all the other pieces would fall into place. "We're looking for Old Gods that had the power to resurrect…" He pointed a finger at Shin. "Sorry open the veil between the worlds…"

"You cannot imagine the amount of gods we are looking for. Also which ones would want apocalypse to happen!?"

The rumbling box sounded strange without there heated conversation.

'Ting'

The doors opened and instantly I felt myself breathing better than I had. Hands reached down and dragged me from the lift carriage.
The moon was high in the sky as I sat with Logan and Shin explaining in detail about Morgana and her gift. How she had tried to get the Fallen, to help her take over the kingdom, and how the Fallen wanted nothing more but to enslave her and use her to their own end.

Logan smiled at the end of the story.

"Thank the earth mother they did not join. Can you imagine what an army that would have been... our ranks would have been slain before our very eyes..."

Shin looked over to the pair of us.
"The others must not know the full truth of where you have obtained this information as they will undoubtedly try and use you again John... or worse... the count still has control over Patricia!"

"Then why haven't we ended him as Luke was supposed to have done."

Logan's eyes seemed sorrowful. "A Fallen of the coming can play amazing mind tricks on all of us... believe me john. I have tried. Ma'beth pulled me out of there a screaming wreck. Even with the enchantments and the ear coverings and the glasses... he just gets inside your head..."

"Well I know one thing that will work... fire..."

*

The following night saw Patricia leave back to Holland. Logan mentioned something about a place called Dance Duivel...

Many of us were sorry to see her go all apart from Sister Abigail who seemed strangely quiet for such an outspoken woman.

Logan entered back into the room from walking Patricia to the escort.

Captain Redman stood and walked around to the board. He pushed out of the way and pressed a button on the wall.

A screen came forward and flickered into life.

"We have a request..."

The screen went bright white and a figure appeared on the screen.
The face of the Imam appeared his face grave with concern. It seemed that his beard had more white than usual.

"John. It is good to see you again… Captain, we have a problem…"

I nodded towards him but knew this was only pleasantries.

The captain moved around the tables and threw out folders to each of us.

I opened the folder and there was a picture of the dried corpse of the girl I had seen in my dream-vision.
Something must have changed in my expression because Rhoswen looked at me. "John…?"

"I'm sorry… this is the girl that was at the ceremony that I saw in regards to the goblet…"

The Imam took a deep breath as though slightly relieved. "The body was found in the Epping Jewish Cemetery. Rabbi Levi is down re-blessing the area…" He went silent for a little while whilst another man approached him with more paperwork. He shuffled and looked up again. "Where are we with these goblets?"

Logan spoke next. "We have some new information regarding the goblets… as we know…" he stood up and walked to the side of Shin Tao. "They were made by the first in the void, although they had no way of getting it through the veil." Shin nodded to Logan.
"It seems that the First and the Fallen have had to make alliances to get the goblets through the void…. The one we have was passed through the veil by Mab…"

The Imam looked at as though bemused. "Mab… that is impossible she is pagan mythology…"

"No matter what you believe, Mab has always been the one in our beliefs that affect the weaker mind. She turns them to her will!" Eselbern was fuming.

"I mean no disrespect to your people Eselbern but find it hard sometimes to believe there is any other than Allah…"

Rhoswen broke into the conversation. "There is much more to our worlds than just one belief… We have spoken before with the order regarding this!"

Her eyes were turning red again.

Sister Abigail slammed her fist on the table. "This is not the time to be arguing!" She straightened her dress and calmly collected the cross from about her neck. "We have managed to capture one of these goblets and we have a fallen to question. Let us use this opportunity to unite and find out where the other five are."

Logan and the others seemed shock to see her reaction. This was obviously not normal behaviour for our dear sister.

The Imam coughed. "I'm sorry for creating any in fighting with your team. I agree sister, we need to concentrate in finding those goblets… may Allah protect you."
His image nodded and the screen went blank.

Ma'beth cracked her knuckles." I've been looking forward to this."

Werner smiled. It was obvious she got to torture; a great many Fallen.

Logan however looked to me. "I think John and I should handle this one… after all, we like them able to talk and no offence the last one you did shatter his jaw…"

I could see a cruel smile emanate around Ma'beth's mouth that made me think that she took far too much pleasure from it

Lust of the fallen

I was glad to get out of the room as the risen argument about whose religion was right or wrong seemed to playing heavily on the occupants.

Logan literally pulled me out before anything could start up again.

"Sorry lad. That gets them in fighting every time. Just glad it wasn't your priest friend. I swear that man does it on purpose."

Down again into the complex we walked. All the while I kept thinking on the girl that had been drained by so many. Is that how my kind were made. How many of them had been human once? Would I participate in something like that if I lost control? I thought back to the blood on my lips. If there was any one I could trust I knew Logan would be the one.

"Logan... Last night..."

"Let me stop you there lad... I think I know what you are going to say?"

"Really... then how?"

"This one we captured last night has no telepathic abilities like our dear count!"

It wasn't the question I was going to ask him, in fact I hadn't even thought about the woman I had lopped of her hand just a few days ago.
"Logan... that wasn't the question I was going to ask... Do I seem different to you?"

Logan went to brush it off however I grabbed hold him and looked into his eyes.

"I can tell you you're an ugly mother fucker who's pissing me off with this cryptic shit?" he laughed then looked me up and down.
"You shaved... no that's not it..." He then proceeded to spin me around in a circle.

"You've got a hicky! Did you get lucky last night?"

I stared deeply into his eyes. He returned the look and smiled wildly.
"Patricia's great isn't she..." He went a little coy. "Of all the women I've been with... I've always had a soft spot for that old girl..." he nudged me and winked.

I could feel myself getting angry for some reason.
"I drank human blood last night...!"

Logan grabbed my skull and forced my eyes as wide as they could go.
After a moment he dipped his head.
When he brought his great shaggy head up and looked at me there was relief and a little sadness in his eyes.

"It was given willingly and you didn't infect the person... I'm guessing you weren't alone with Patricia last night? Was it one of the guards?"

I started walking away from Logan. Could I tell him that it was Sister Abigail! Would it jeopardise her and her position.
"Hey buddy it's me... I just need to know. Just in case they have something. I mean let's be honest. I doubt a girl with her record hasn't got something. As for you and me, well I'm half human so my other side kills those things for me. As for you... well you are... kinda... different!"

He dipped his head and then looked up at me with his cats eyes on show. It looked like a kitten pleading for food.

"It's... Sister Abigail..."

*

Logan and I walked toward the cell in which the woman Fallen was. Logan had been quiet the entire time. I think he was in shock by the idea that sister Abigail could have been in participation.

The guards outside the room stood to attention as the approached.

"How is she today mike?"

"As foul mouthed as usual Sir." He looked at me with a tiny part of suspicion lingering in his eyes.

"Is she chained/?"

"All apart from her stump!" He nodded towards me. That was a good bit of fighting you did the other night sir..."

"Thanks…" I saw the doubt was leaving his eyes in regards to his fear of me.

"Right let's go see her."

Logan took lead into the small room that she had neem put in.

"Lights please gents.

The light flickered into life and there hanging by only three limbs was the girl who had tried to take his head off last night.

. She saw me and hawked at her throat. The largest piece of phlegm she could muster.

"Traitor…" The phlegm landed just shy of my feet,

I turned to Logan. "I see her hand is has had some editions…"

"I really must speak to Ma'beth about that. Damn girl loves to soften people up…"

I looked towards my boot then back at Logan. "Huh… could have fooled me."

Logan walked calmly towards her. "Do you have any idea how many of your kind I have made into ash and mush?"

He grabbed her chin firmly and turned her face towards him. "You should know by now that my people are immune to being turned" He let go of her chin.

I looked towards Logan. I guess my look said it all.

"Oh yeah 'cause we don't follow your rules; our people can still die but we are not affected by the same curse…" he turned his hand that gradually grew more into a paw.
"We have our own curse!"

I got closer to Logan. "I didn't know that!"

"Tell you about it later…" He turned back to the girl. "So I'm going to ask nicely… where did you get the goblet and where are the other five?"

She looked at me, her eyes jet black but I could feel the loathing that lay in her eyes.

"Do want you want but you'll never get the information you want!"

Logan signalled to the trooper standing by the door. He knocked on the door.

Another trooper backed into the room, towing a metal table arrayed in different symbols.
Logan pulled the tray around to face her.

"Mmm... what haven't I tried yet... well this was a fun tool." He picked up a long silver spike laden with different symbols. Without blinking he drove it into her stomach. Her mouth fell open in a silent scream.

"How does that feel?"

She gasped for breath as I could feel the pain emanate within her. She turned her head towards me as though the hate in her was being mixed with cries of fear.

Slowly Logan passed his hand over the table. It was calculating the way he did it. He turned and looked at me.
"You see John. The true torture is not one that is done with the body but one that is done through the mind. It's best I teach you now as you will most probably

out live me." He smiled but I could tell he wasn't truly enjoying what he was doing.

"You know I don't feel half as much enjoyment as I did when I tortured the last werewolf…"

His hand stopped at another implement. The implement was shaped similar to the knife I had seen of the priests use to slice open its victim.
He picked it up and waved it in front of the Fallen.

"Do you recognise this…?" his eyes intently looking at her face.

Although the agony was still flowing through her he could see something I couldn't.

"Yes. I have met one of your priests… I took great joy in handing him over to the order. I believe his screams were echoing in this same room. He begged your god for forgiveness before he was sent to the nether realm…"

She tried desperately to speak. "I don't know anything…"

Logan picked up the knife and run it down her clothes allowing them to open. Her naked body stirred something within me.

Do you like what you see…? John…

I shook my head; somehow she was talking to me.

"Logan…" My voice faint, as though it were distant.

You know you want me… Just kill him and we can feast on the humans within this base together…

Logan looked at me. "Should I leave you two alone?"

He seemed to recognise what was going on.

Release me and I will help you change to what you should be…. I can feel you have been with one of us before and I know you long to have my touch upon you…

I pulled Logan to the side.
"She is talking to me Logan. I can hear her in my head… she wants…"

"This is usual. All Angels crave what humans have. Intimacy!"

Logan dropped the knife to the table with a clatter.

"Robertson. Take this back out… We'll go and give John a chance; on his own…"

Robertson pulled the tray from the room and Logan followed after it.

The lights in the room went out and I saw in the bi colour tone her supple body.

Come and take me John. I can show you what it's like to be one of us…

I walked as though pulled towards her and reached out and pulled the ropes that bound her from the truss that held her.

That's it… Feel my body against you…

She fell against me, weak in body. Her missing hand felt strange. Her mouth fell against my neck as she slumped upon me. The next thing I knew her teeth entered my neck drawing upon my life's fluid.

I stumbled and she fell against me onto the floor.

She released her teeth and her hand that had been chopped off started to reform.

You see… I can come become whole as soon as I have fed. You can do the same…

Her hands drawing over my body and up to my hair. She stroked through my lengthening hair and began to kiss strongly against my lips.

I felt you wanted me the first time we met...

She propped herself up upon me. Ripping the clothes that covered my body until my chest was bare.
She dragged her nails up from my belly button to my sternum. I felt the warm hot blood seep from the scratch. She licked up wards, the feeling heightening my sexual desire for this woman.

She flicked her hair as she lifted back up from me.

You taste all holy... who have you had recently..

She reached down to my belt and pulled the leather so much that it ripped in two. Her chest heaving, her nipples pert; she seemed to know what I was thinking.

She leant them closer to me so that the nipple entered my mouth. I licked around it involuntary, my teeth lengthening as it nipped the skin. The blood trickled from it and into my mouth. The taste sweet and salty.
She forced the breast into my face forcing it closer to my teeth. I sank them in as I felt and heard her moan in pleasure as the blood trickled into me.
I felt my body arousing further.
She stroked my face and I let go. Her face; soft and desirable.

She moved her slender hands down towards my groin, soft at first and then getting frustrated as the jean material not giving so easily.
She pulled her body down so that her head was level with my groin. It throbbed in the intense feeling of her being so close to me.
She plunged her teeth into my jeans and practically ripped the material from my throbbing member. Her hands stoking gently; then her tongue licking upwards.

Then her teeth drove into my member. I squealed in pain and pleasure.

Slowly I could feel myself wanting her more and more.

She lifted herself off of me and spread her wings out from behind her. Her naked body inviting, seductive.

Join me John…

I stood up and let my clothes drop away from me. My wings out I rushed towards her driving her against the wall. She squirmed with pleasure at the force of which I forced her against the wall.

Take me…

I pinned her hands against the wall and she pulled her legs up to wrap around my waist. I entered her with the same force that I forced her against the wall. Pushing harder and harder with the beat of a heartbeat. Her wings wrapping around me. I felt deeper within her, with every thrust I heard her whimper...

That's when it happened.

η

The confession in passion

I walked unsteadily from the room. The woman's body lay asleep enfolded within its wings.

The troops grinning when I exited the room told me I was not alone in last night.
One even winked at me as I walked along the corridor.

Brother Simeon was the first to approach me after the night's activities.

"John... John.... I wanted to speak with you…"

His robes sweeping the floor, as he run.

I carried on walking toward my bedroom. I was tired and the information that sat in my head was still swimming about disjointed. I was sure a sleep would help me figure out what all the images would mean.

Finally his shuffling feet reached me and he placed a hand upon my naked shoulder.

"John…"

I turned around and looked at Brother Simeon. Something made him step back.

"Look, brother… I gotta get some sleep 'cause I'm feeling dead at the moment…"

He chuckled at the remark.

"That's good John… I didn't think that you would retain this much humour after… Erm…"

It must have been the way I looked at him that made him falter.

"Look John… I just want to go through what you've seen. No matter how bad it is… I just want to sit down and go through what… oh yes… please we can do it in your quarters…"

I carried on walking and turned into my quarters. The dutiful Brother followed me. His pencil and book appearing from his robes.

"Now go through what you remember…"

I threw my body into full long into the cot. My hands covered my eyes.

Brother Simeon sat down on the chair I threw my clothes upon.

"So John…" the gentle scribbling of paper was soothing somehow. "Tell me what you saw…"

I sighed knowing that he wasn't going to give up with the questions.

The countess stood before a group of caravans…. A man approached her. His voice heavily accented in Irish. He was bowing elaborately as though to mock her presence. She asked him about his strength of numbers.

They didn't state a number exactly only that there were enough.
She took a drink of blood with them. I noticed that all around them were pictures of Magpies.

The next image was one of a dark cavern. There was murmuring all around. It felt deep as though we were within some caves.
The fires glowed purple as though they were not real fire.
A man in the same robes of those of the dark priests gathered around steam coming from a pot.

The countess was there again talking happily with the priests. I could feel the Firsts within the deep walls. The symbols on the walls were daemonic and there priests I could see hungered for the countess in a strange way. It wasn't lust it was something else. Similar to jealousy.

A Goblet was presented to the countess. It had another marking on it, I couldn't make out what it was properly but something told me it was a different to Mab's mark.

Another scene opened up; it was freezing. The light was minimal; air froze mid breath and hung like a cloud of fog.

I could feel the ice forming upon my face. A mounded snow formation had smoke billowing from the top of it. A door swung open and inside a fire sat in the middle of the rounded room.

When we went inside we felt the smoke fill our lungs. An old woman dept in furs of deer huddled about the room. Wooden symbols hung down from the ceiling making it impossible to stand upright. She smelled of deer blood and fat. Her teeth brown from a root she was chewing.

At first she seemed to not notice us in the room but eventually waved us closer. The countess got as close as she dared to the fire.

The old woman turned and with a lunge she threw the goblet into her arms.

The symbols on the cup were of three triangles of sorts.

"Is that it...? John..."

"Please brother... let me rest... I have told you everything I can for now..." the room began to spin and before I knew it the darkness was upon me.

*

When I awoke the room was dark and the chair which the Brother had sat was vacated apart from a bottle upon it.

A note sate upon the chair.

Good work last night... Even Ma'beth was impressed. Have a drink on us.
L

I pulled the cork from the bottle. The smell of the blood filled my nostrils and my teeth and stomach longed for its fulfilling sustenance.

*

The briefing room was sat ready for my arrival..
Logan looked at me and mimicked wiping my chin.
I realised that I had still blood on my lips.

Captain Redman watched me sit and then began his briefing.

"Brother Simeon has told us what you have... err... revealed from your interrogation… 'Ahem'…" He shuffled his papers as though he felt awkward about the way the interrogation was conducted.
"He has highlighted one area that I believe…" he nodded towards Logan and Werner. "You know who they are!"

Werner stood this time instead of Logan.
"The Magpie you say about, they are one of the clans which were lured into Morgana's plot… you have to understand… these are our prey…"

I looked towards Logan to which he nodded at me.

"Then I guess we'd better start there..."

A commotion erupted outside of the door. A trooper run in. I recognised Robertson straight away.

"Sir... it's her... she's escaped..."

Ma'beth was the first one to her feet. She ran out of the room at full speed in her cat form. Followed swiftly by Rhoswen.

The only one who seemed stuck to his seat was Brother Simeon.

Troops crowded the halls running back and forth.
"Captain... what are your troops carrying to stop her..." Mid stride he produced a different gun from a holster.

"It's not near as affective as you guys but it emits a high yield light which has been known to cut holes in people like you..."

I nodded at him and then left him behind as I headed towards my room.

I grabbed Saqit.

As I ran through the hallways the troops seemed to be moving so slowly that they seemed almost freeze framed as I went passed them.

I caught up with Logan who was at full leaping towards the main entrance.

"We can't let her leave John… She knows our location and I think one of the guards let slip that the count was with us too…"

"Where's Rhoswen and Ma'beth?"

He sniffed at the air… "She's up ahead… get up there and help. You'll get there quicker than I will…"

With a renewed boost I ran quicker through the halls. Almost floating about them.

The night air was refreshing. Ma'beth was swatting with her massive paws at something that was close to a tree.

Rhoswen seemed too shapeless as she moved. Her eyes glowing red in the night.

I flew at the woman… at first I think she thought I was coming to help her. It was upon the first strike that she realised I wasn't.

She flew off to the side cackling at me as though she were a witch.

"You petty excuse for man… you think that you can get lucky again…"
She pulled one of the light guns from her clothing at aimed it at me. The light began to cut through my wing.
I spiralled to the floor.

As I hit the floor Logan pounced over me and lunged toward the woman.
She merely swerved out of his way.

It was like watching a cat leaping at the moths in the night.
Every now and then she swooped down and grabbed a trooper and pulled them into the air ripping through there clothing and feasting on their blood. Their bodies soon started to pile up around us.

The fallen feasted as though they were simply an open buffet.

Eselbeth glowed white in the darkness of the night. Her robes radiated a strange illuminance; as though the moon reflected the light of the sun.

Sister Abigail stepped out from behind her. I saw a long bow pulled taught and from it flew and flaming arrow. It struck straight into her chest.
I looked back to Eselbeth and saw her chanting and drawing her hands apart as though she were expanding something.
The Fallen engulfed in the flames that original started at her chest. Her embers began to fall into the silent air.

Cheers went up into the night but all I heard were the silent screams of the Fallen as she flaked into the night sky.

The Gathering

As the troops gathered in the main entrance way filing into the green trucks that stood waiting to move out. I could see the happiness they felt from the previous nights encounter, but I saw something also troubled them,

Rhoswen walked up behind me and touched lightly on my shoulder.
"You seem troubled... What it is that you are thinking?"
I turned to her, she seemed different to how she was normally, more relaxed than usual.

I stuttered. "The troops are... saddened..."

"They lost a number of friends last night when that woman escaped... Their funerals where today."

"Oh... and I didn't realise... I thought they would turn and join our ranks again as fallen!"

"It doesn't work that way… john. You are special when it comes to Fallen. They fear what there brothers in arms would turn out like. I don't know if you know this but Robertson was one of them."

I remembered his smiling face and his kindly nature towards me.

Rhoswen looked at me. Her face indescribable.

"When a trooper falls to a fallen or to any other… Disease… then they have to take precautions...!"

"I'm sorry what precautions."

Rhoswen looked at me, her eyes deeper than any human should be. "They kill them. Dismember them and then bury them of course…"

She walked off toward Ma'beth. The way she stroked her hair as she turned up reminded me of the way a human loves a cat.

Logan and Brother Simeon walked through the door.

"John... grab your gear... tonight! We hunt!"

*

The trucks rolled through the quiet streets of small villages. There seemed to be at least ten trucks behind our one. The difference was that the truck I was within was a hard top with all sides covered in UV shielding. The troops however sat in the soft top four tonners.

"A contingent of our brothers will be joining us tonight." Werner spoke from his chair. His finger nails scratching at the arms of the front seat. Logan turned from the driving seat.

"You're going to love these guys!" He grinned into the rear view mirror.

I sat back in the chair; Saqit sat ladle in my lap.
"Logan... I've met one of these werewolves once before. It tried to kill my wife and child..."

Ma'beth sat opposite me; her face contorted in rage. "When did this happen?"

Rhoswen placed a hand on her shoulder to calm her.

I looked towards the others. They all seemed disturbed by the news.

"It chased me into the church where I was changed. Then I saw it try and kill my family... that's when I..."

"Logan this cannot be coincidence... how long have the Fallen been working with the wolves...?" Ma'beth's teeth gritted as she spoke.

It was not Logan who spoke but Eselbeth.

"The Fallen and the wolves started truly working together, during the Second World War... Did you not read up on your own famous clan member...? Rose Wolbear?"

Rhoswen looked towards Ma'beth. It seemed the name seemed to focus the two together.

"She is my Grandmother!"

The whole truck went silent for a while. Sister Abigail who strangely had joined us in the truck was the first to speak up.

"It was Rose Wolbear who first bartered the treaty with the Order and the marked back in nineteen forty-two..." she pointed toward Rhoswen.

"Your Grandmother was also the first to join forces with your kind... Although the information is sketchy I believe Grandmother saved a Faere in the woods of Bavaria upon the first German incursion.

I looked up. "Patricia mentioned that the count and countess were working with the Germans and also many that wore the wolf mark..."

"Yes the first real alliance was born there. Although the union of the two races have been frayed over the years from both sides; despising each other..."
The truck fell silent once more but I felt there were still many unanswered questions buzzing around each other's minds; like a hive of bees disturbed by a whiff of a hornet.

*

The trucks came to a halt just shy of a small town in the midlands. I saw signs for Telford out of the front windscreen. I saw a great fire burning in the distance.

'BANG BANG'

The side of the truck rattled as though being hit with a battering ram.

As the door lowered, I saw at least twenty men and women standing in clothing made of hessian. Logan came through from the front and fell into the arms of the woman in front.

"It is so good to see you again my Brother!"

Logan released his grasp and lead the woman and the group into the back of the truck.

"John. I want you to meet my new old friend... Raquel... Raquel Wolhawk..."

"Hi John..." Her hand extended although I could see she was wary of me as her eyes had already changed to the slit cat like eyes I was so accustomed to seeing.

"Uh... Hi..." I moved Saqit to the side of me.

She leaned in kissed both cheeks.

"Don't mind our dear Raquel. She's Danish and has a wonderful greeting..." Raquel released me slapped Logan's backside.

I heard her shout over Logan's shoulder. "Werner you old tom cat... get out of my chair..." She had a lovely sense of humour.

The other marked boarded the truck and the doors lifted again.

"Logan... you never said where our prey is?" One the marked asked.

"Oh Barry I forgot you were here with us." He smiled back at him. "We're going to the coast. Near to Durdle Door..."

Barry gave a thumbs up and took his seat along the side of the truck.

The truck resumed its travel, as the morning light blessed the windscreen I looked upon it in longing through the UV screen. Will I ever be able to see the light of the sun again without it ending my life?

*

The convoy took only a few stops on the way at a few service stations. I heard the joy of the troops jumping off to run and get scrum.

Logan got back in with a heaped bag of burgers.
"Oh John... I forgot. There's a bottle of something sweet for you. Patricia said she thought you would like a holy tipple..."

The sister seemed bashful at this statement and I saw her look diverting her gaze whenever I looked in her direction.

"Logan... I completely forgot!" Raquel who sat happy in the front seat of the truck passed a battered letter from her person.

Logan placed his burger to the side and unfolded the letter. I saw in the mirror tears rolling down his cheek. He almost roared in joy. "I have a son!"

The clapping throughout the truck increased the banter.

"You fucking lucky bastard..."

"Didn't think your salmon could swim the right way after the shit you smoke...!"

An girl in her fifties who looked different to the others spoke up.
"Logan... Is that Rose's daughter boy?"

"It is Rientje... Raquel... you been reading my letters again?"

"Don't look at me... Rientje probably got a letter herself from Rose..."

Rhoswen spoke up. "You have a letter from Grandmother?"

"His names Ethan after my father... he's your half brother now...!" Said Logan.

"Has he... the mark?" It was Rientje who asked the question.

His tears were in full flow but this time it seemed to be mixed with sadness. I couldn't understand how having their mark would be bring such sadness.

Barry piped up. "Let's hope he takes after his mothers... cause you an ugly bastard!"

The entire truck burst with laughter.

The truck started up again and soon we were on our way again.

*

The sun began to fall as the signs for Lulworth cove and Bovington Camp came into view.

I could feel the intense flowing through everyone in the truck. It felt like fear. It was so strong that I could almost taste it on the air.

The truck pulled off the main road and passed a triangular sign with a tank in it.

It rocked violently until a it reached a copse.

The noise of the other trucks emptying seemed to signal the inhabitants to crowd toward the door.

I carried on sitting facing the door. Whilst the others poured out like ants, from a hill.

θ

Hunting Dogs

It was strange to see such a bizarre combination of people. Four trucks lined up behind each other. The accents combined seemed to echo in the night.

"Aren't we a bit... noisy?"
I stood next to Werner.

He looked at me and nodded. "Don't you worry we are some miles away and the dogs cannot hear us till..." He pointed up into the clear night sky.
"The moon rises; unlike us... they need it to change their forms!"

I nodded to Werner and walked off to see the different groups.

The marked all seemed to be huddled around a small fire. The older woman sat nearest the fire, a pot of ash and water in one hand as she marked each of her tribe with different symbols. I saw Logan, Ma'beth and Werner all heading towards them.

A group of troops stood around one of the trucks. Their voices portrayed them as American. Within the cab of the same truck sat Captain Redman. His pen and paper, scribbling down notes.

Another group; much smaller than the first were sitting cleaning their rifles and talking in low voices. As I got closer to them I realised that they were British. There emblems upon their shoulders showed they were Special Forces.

Sister Abigail walked up to me.

"I notice you are seeing their insignia... John they are here for a special purpose.... Please come meet them!"

I walked over with her and the men jumped to attention at her approach.

"At ease gentleman... Charles... good to see you again!"

"Ma'am" he tipped his hat towards her.

"John... Charles and his men here are tasked with search and recovery of our next Goblet..."

I turned to the Sister. "But the goblet... its effects..."

"Sir... I've gone over this with the sister here. You are our VIP on this mission. We've read the report and it states that you are not affected by its powers. Once we have it then we're to escort you back here."

The other troops continued loading there magazines with shining bullets.

"Silver bullets?" I raised an eyebrow at the commander.

"We've had quite a few encounters with these beasty's sir... we found that bullet needs a lot of power to go in but needs to stop shy of leaving else they will just get back up again...!"

One of the squad handed me the bullet and I noticed it was etched in a star of david formation.

When I handed it back the man looked at me and mimicked the bullet hitting and exploding into little pieces.

Whistles echoed into the night air.

"Sir... 'tis best you join us for this..." he turned to the sister. "Are you joining us tonight Ma'am?"

"No Charles. I'm going to have enough trouble tonight patching up the Americans..." She smiled and walked back to the UV truck.

I followed behind to the third truck. It had been littered with spotlights.

Captain Redman stood with his note pad open.

"Members of my troop will proceed along the beach, west of Lulworth Cove hitting there beach, where the werewolves are camped..." He pointed towards Logan. "I suggest you take your people up to the ridge line and descend from above..."

He nodded towards Charles. "Captain... take your troop further west and approach from the rear of the encampment."
He spread out a large photographic print and started drawing on it with a red pen. He circled a number of caravans far to the west.
"If I'm right, this is where we are looking..."

Charles spoke up. "Sir. What numbers were reported this morning by the spotter plane that took this?"

"No more than fifty adults..."

A distant howl took the troops by surprise.

"I think it's time we foxtrot Oscar... don't you captain..." Logan smiled and winked at Charles.

There was something between them that I couldn't figure out.

*

I followed Charles and his men on a large sweep around towards Bat's head. They jaunted along the winding roads as though it were light morning run.

As we passed the turning for the road to Durdle door we heard the howling again. This time it was joined by others. When I listened carefully I was sure that there were more than the fifty dogs howling.

Charles held up his hand and everyone but me; stopped. I crashed into the man in front.

The next moment as I went to apologise I realised I was on my own.
I sniffed the air and looked around but the bushes on each side of the road seemed exactly as they should.

I wasn't sure if it would work but I tried to listen as hard as I could. That's when I heard it. The panting!

I pulled Saqit from the holder on my back and spread my wings. With a push and a jump I looked around the landscape. A group of Werewolves were gathering up the road. There heartbeats throbbing in my ears. There were at least ten of them. They were sniffing the air as though they were searching for something.

They lolloped down the road. Unsure of whether they should walk on all fours or just on two.

I allowed myself to touch back down. The blade shone strangely in the light of the moon.

The sound of their heartbeats and the panting of their breath become unbearable. Something inside of me just wanted to rip their jaws apart.

I started walking forward; they spotted me and I could see their eyes looking at me as though puzzled. That was until I flicked Saqit around in front of me.

A low rumbling growl issued from their throats. They took five steps towards me and then in unison I saw their heads explode as though someone had set a firework off inside there brain. It was preceded with a fut. fut. noise.

Out of the bushes trod Charles and his team.
Charles hand went back up and signalled for his troops to move on.

"Listen... John. I need you to go and warn the others... This feels like a set up.!"

More howls came from the Durdle door.

"We have little time... John we'll proceed just get over there and see what you can do!"

I nodded and took flight.

The wind rushed through my hair as I beat my leathered wings as hard as I could. I passed over the fields and below I could see clusters of wolves making their way towards the beach. I pushed on.

Ahead I could see the catlike forms of the marked they were beginning there descent towards the beach.
I flew lower until I was close enough to yell.

"It's a trap...!"

Logan came back into form.

"John... what the hell you doing here...?"

"There's no time... your being surrounded... There isn't fifty of them... there's five hundred!"

Almost on queue a howl began from the west spreading all around them.

"John... Find us a way out then contact the Americans. Do what you can to get as many of them out!"

Once more I rose above the ground flying higher and looking into the night's landscape. The only area the wolves had as yet not covered was a path to the west of the Man O 'War Beach.

I floated back down and signalled to the marked as to where the weakest exit was and took off toward the landing party.

The Americans had already landed and the scene was devastating. Limbs lay on the ground whilst several werewolves plunged their snouts within the carcasses of the bodies. The troopers were somehow still screaming as there intestines were being ripped out.
I noticed a group being enveloped.

I swooped in feeling Saqit energising in my hands. I began to allow it to move the way it wanted. It was as though it could feel what I needed to do. The blades arced around my body. The first wolf to see me lunged forward on all paws. Its ugly snout snarling and drooling with blood soaked teeth. The repugnant smell of its mouth made me want to wretch. Saqit spun in my hands and brought up with swift stroke. The head parted in the middle, a shocked look in its eyes as the jaw and head parted and for a moment it was like freeze frame showing the brain and tongue in a perfect cross section. The body fell to the floor and I stepped over it. My feet slipping in its blood.

Three more wolves turned away from the spray of bullets coming from the group of Americans.

Saqit forced my body round and I turned with her and she cleaved limbs from limbs. Noses from heads and spliced through the chests revealing the beating heart within.

I saw Captain Redman within the crowd.

"Where's your boats captain?"

I turned; or rather Saqit turned me just in time to strike the head from a wolf.

"We're cut off John... what can you do for us?"

"Get as close as you can to the water... I'll bring you a boat!"
As I turned I felt Saqit swirl around my body and another slump at my feet.

The wolves were crowding over the beach. I could see in their eyes that they weren't just mindless animals they were working together in a pack. Decimating and communicating as feasted on the troops.

I grabbed the nearest dingy and pushed it into the water. Using my wings to push it along the surf.
The troops were already piling into the water. Falling over each other; just to get to the boat.

I pulled it as close as I could then grabbed the captain and threw him in the boat.

"Get my men... please John..."

I grabbed as many as I could from jaws of the wolves.

I looked around at the black and white picture of the beach and smelt the blood on the sand. My hunger returned with vengeance... I feel to my knees and the salt water washed over me.

I heard the noise of the engines roar into life and saw the boat make its way away from the beach.

In that moment I thought of Logan. I took off once more towards the retreating marked ones.

I knew that the wolves now starved of their prey would soon go after Logan and his group.

I found them on the beach of the Man O 'war. Bodies lay crumpled and ripped to shreds as I hovered over the scene.

The woman Rientje seemed lit from within and with each step the wolves took a huge wave would hit the beach and drag a number of wolves with them.

I flew down in time to decapitate the wolf waiting to strike Logan. The wolf's head rolled to the side.

"We need to get you out of here Logan..." He looked at me dazed and confused. Blood rippled down his fur.

A rock pool behind them swirled with furious speed and Rhoswen appeared from the water.

"Over here... NOW!"

I grabbed Logan by the shoulder and dragged his semi limp form to the rock pool.

Turning and pushing the wolves back with the slices and thrusts of Saqit.

As I turned back I saw Logan and the few remaining slip into the swirling water. However Rhoswen was knelt by a lone body being pushed by the water.

I realised it was Ma'beth.

In a fit of anger she gathered up water from all around her and threw it towards the hoard of wolves bearing down upon her. It were as though she threw daggers, because each wolf the water hit seemed to take away that part of them.

Arms and heads and chests re-appeared washing up on the beach the other side of the hoard.

Rhoswen pulled the body of Ma'beth closer to her and together they swirled away.

*

When I returned; Captain Redman was ushering all back onto the trucks.

Logan was being nursed by sister Abigail.
Werner was scratching the sides of the truck.
Rientje and Raquel were the only ones to have returned; from the initial twenty that joined us.

Out of the darkness a call went out.

"HALT... FRIEND... OR FOE?"

"FRIEND!"

"ADVANCE ONE AND BE RECOGNISED."

I heard the loading mechanism go forward on a heavy machine gun.

"Captain"

From the darkness walked the team I had originally gone out with. They held a box between two, it was an old fashioned wooden crate.

Charles walked up to me whilst his men loaded the crate on the back of the truck...

He winked at me. "Got it..."

*

Raquel now in the driving seat; with Logan sat next to Werner. Logan's arm draped around Werner, comforting him.

"Logan... what will they say of this day..."

"We are story tellers and tell we shall; for those stories are ours, until others repeat them in years to come; for then they can change it for we will not be there to listen..." said Logan with a sorrowful tone.

Epilogue

The return to the base was solemn. No one spoke within the truck. I saw Sister Abigail toil over different soldiers who were injured by the onslaught.
She went between them, sometimes she would shake her head to Eselbeth and Eselbeth would write down on a scrap a paper their name and number.

Later she confided in me that those written down where ones that were infected. Unlike the ones taken by the Fallen these ones would be sent to another part of the country to live out their lives in peace.

Rhoswen did not return to the base until a week after. Her eyes now crimson red.

Although the main funeral's for the troops were held in the day. The bodies of the Marked where sent off in the evening which meant I could at least join them in their sorrow.

Werner stepped forward to the head of those present. He was wrapped in the skin of a wolf he had slain. He looked sorrowful and angry yet something more. "You who now go to mother earth do so with our thanks. For without you we may not be here to continue the fight we have been given..."

His voice crackling slightly as he spoke.

"I have been recalled by the clan. My father is dying and I must take upon his mantle..."

Logan stepped forward and placed his hand upon Werner's broad shoulder.

Rientje stepped forward to the pyres that sat with each of the bodies of the Marked.

In the corner of my eye I could see the silhouette of Rhoswen standing in the shadow, however; I saw others standing with her.

Rientje raised her hand and said aloud.

*"We are the Marked,
From earth we come and to earth we go.
The fire represents our life.
Strong and proud!
Our sisters,
And brothers, we will ne'er forget."*

She went to step forward with a flaming branch but stopped just short of Ma'beth's body.

"Rose...?"

Lastly a little note from me the Author...

Well I wanted to say thank you for actually reading this bit... but if you didn't you won't realise this isn't the end.
John the main character speaks of hunger and pain and loss.
The order of Ezekial series will continue...

The characters in this story are not linked to any real person, so if I killed someone with your name. Don't feel it's a personal thing...

Dedication of this...

I'd like to dedicate this to my family and friends who put up with me speaking about nothing but my writing adventures.

Special mention

Rose – My Grandmother I wish we had more time together.

Leeann – My Wife for giving me time to finish what I have started.

To my sons – Never give up on a dream. Persevere endure but never give up!

Sarah – For being my Beta Reader! ☺

Laura from justpublishit.com for an amazing front cover!!

Crystal and Cayce – For helping me with the blurb!! You guys are fantastic!!

Inside info

For hints of what is going to happen in the next story come join me Facebook SIG SciFi Stories or Twitter @SIGStories

Other stories:

The Last Shadow Warrior Book 1
The Last Shadow Warrior Book 2

Shorts

Past Memories: Cradle to Grave
Fear, Helplessness and Chains
Spawn of the Net

Poetry

Poetry from a Twisted Bard

Lastly... lastly

Check out Wattpad for Rose Wolbear the ongoing prequel to Wolfsbane and Fallen Angel Am I!!

Made in the USA
Charleston, SC
07 November 2016